Rumba, salsa, ___

They're here! T___ ___ ___ our special danc___ ___ up *Alexandra's L___* ___ ___ ___ ...ore than five hundre___ ___ ___ ___ on board, hoping to improve their moves with some of the most talented dance instructors in the field today.

For those passengers who aren't part of the dance group, the themed cruise still has lots to offer. Check the newsletter daily to find out times and places for dance demonstrations and competitions. Ball gowns and tuxes are the order of the day, so be prepared for a whirling kaleidoscope of color and style that will rival a Vegas show.

Is the Latin beat too hot for your blood? A sedate waltz more your style than a sultry tango? Then come up to the Polaris Lounge and dance to the gentler tunes of Glenn Miller. Don't have a partner? Our gentleman hosts are there to glide you across the dance floor.

The only rule is to have fun! The staff of *Alexandra's Dream* offers you glamour and adventure as we sail the waters of the Caribbean. We want this cruise to be one you'll never forget.

MARCIA KING-GAMBLE

is a Caribbean-American novelist who makes two coasts home. A former travel industry executive, Marcia has seen most of the world. The Far East, Venice and New Zealand are three of her favorites.

When not writing or traveling, this bestselling author works off excess energy taking Zumba and kickboxing classes. She indulges her passion for anything old by rummaging through estate sales and antique stores.

Marcia writes for several Harlequin imprints. She loves hearing from readers.

Mediterranean
NIGHTS™

Marcia King-Gamble

THE WAY
HE MOVES

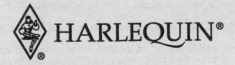

HARLEQUIN®

TORONTO • NEW YORK • LONDON
AMSTERDAM • PARIS • SYDNEY • HAMBURG
STOCKHOLM • ATHENS • TOKYO • MILAN • MADRID
PRAGUE • WARSAW • BUDAPEST • AUCKLAND

ISBN-13: 978-0-373-38971-1
ISBN-10:   0-373-38971-X

THE WAY HE MOVES

Dear Reader,

According to marketing research, less than 10 percent of the American population has actually taken a cruise. This is especially perplexing given cruising is one of the least expensive vacations there is.

There is no other vacation experience as stress free as cruising. You board a ship, unpack your bags and get waited on hand and foot. As an added bonus, you get to visit the countries of your choice, plus enjoy exotic cuisine and world-class entertainment. No getting on and off planes and moving from hotel to hotel. Where else can you have lodging, food and entertainment inclusive in the original price? Am I starting to sound like an infomercial yet?

For almost thirteen years I worked in the cruise industry in an executive capacity. Ships were my life. Anything can happen on a floating city, especially when you have thousands of passengers on board. Believe me, there are literally thousands of stories to tell.

That said, I hope your journey was an informative one. Perhaps you've learned a little about cruising and become interested in visiting a new country. Perhaps your interest in cruising has just been piqued.

If you have questions about cruising, general comments, or just want to say hi, shoot an e-mail my way at mkinggambl@aol.com. Snail mail correspondence should be sent to P.O. Box 25143, Fort Lauderdale, FL 33320.

Happy cruising!

Romantically yours,

Marcia King-Gamble
www.lovemarcia.com

**With grateful thanks to Gordon Buck
for sharing his operational knowledge. Without his
expertise this book would not have been possible.**

DON'T MISS THE STORIES OF

Mediterranean NIGHTS™

CHAPTER ONE

"CALL ME THE MOMENT that pendant is found, *capisce?*"

Tracy Irvine's grip tightened around the receiver. She could tell her ex-husband was losing patience with her. This was her last chance and she needed to deliver or else.

Previously she'd screwed up badly and she might not have another chance to redeem herself. Her child's well-being was at stake here, so she needed to play Sal's sick game. It was the only way to get Franco back. He was her son, their son, and her reason for living.

"I will, Sal, I promise," she said, striving to sound confident. "I won't disappoint you this time."

"You better not, *bella,* especially if you know what's good for you. This is your last chance. There will be hell to pay if you don't deliver this time around." Sal's raucous laughter resounded in her ear.

"When will I get to see Franco?" Tracy asked, trying to hold back the tears that were welling. If Sal knew she was close to breaking, he would get uglier. He had a sadistic streak to him.

"In good time, as soon as that pendant is mine."

"I'll get it for you. I swear I will."

"Do that, *bella,* and soon."

The receiver clunked down, the dial tone reverberating in her ear.

Tracy allowed herself a good cry, then taking a deep breath pulled herself together. In ten minutes she was on duty, greeting passengers as they boarded *Alexandra's Dream.* She'd been hired as a dancer on the cruise ship, but in her off time she performed other duties. Today she was assigned to welcome passengers boarding at Port Everglades in Fort Lauderdale.

No matter how distraught she felt, she had no choice but to look perky.

IN THE EMBARKATION AREA, VIP passengers were being escorted on board. Serena d'Andrea, accompanied by her best friend, Pia Fischer, stepped off the ramp and onto the cruise ship *Alexandra's Dream.* Although Serena was no stranger to the good life, she gaped at the opulent lobby with its elaborate chandeliers and winding staircases leading to an upper deck.

She certainly hadn't been expecting the interior of the luxury vessel to look like a five-star hotel. Her friend Pia seemed equally awed. She used the pamphlet handed to her by the embarkation staff to fan her face.

"Oh, my," Pia gushed, speaking in English instead of their native Spanish. "Oh, my."

"Awesome, as the Americans would say."

Pia nodded her blonde head. "To die for, awesome."

An attractive, brunette crewmember, outfitted in a navy blazer and white slacks, scrutinized their boarding passes before handing them back.

"Welcome aboard, Dr. Fischer and Ms. d'Andrea," the woman said, her dazzling smile washing over them. "You are in one of our penthouse suites. Let me introduce you to your attendant, who will escort you to Zeus Deck."

"My pleasure, ladies." A woman dressed in a black taffeta dress and frilly white apron, stepped forward.

"Gracias," Serena answered, catching herself and quickly switching to English. She was no longer in Argentina and should stick to the language most commonly spoken.

Pia seemed to be making the transition to English much more easily. "I am so looking forward to these next fourteen days," she said. "I plan on catching up on my reading and relaxing every chance I get."

"What about dancing?" Serena reminded her. "Isn't that why we signed up for this charter? We came aboard to perfect our rhythm steps and take instructions from professional dancers."

Pia flung an arm around Serena's shoulders.

"Of course we'll dance every chance we get. I'm just glad to be away from patients and their issues. After a while you get burned out."

Serena nodded her understanding. She knew

exactly what Pia meant. Emotionally she was exhausted and had been for the last six months.

The two were as opposite as two people could be. Pia, a well respected psychiatrist, was petite and blonde with a chic pixie haircut and a vivacious personality that inspired instant trust. She and Serena, the more reserved of the two, had been best friends since nursery school. Serena was tall, with thick, dark wavy hair and wide violet eyes.

The doors of an elevator opened and the maid waved them in. The glass elevator whizzed them up several floors before stopping on ten.

"Zeus Deck," the attendant announced, pointing to a discreet gilt plaque on the wall when they got off. After a short walk down a plush carpeted hallway, the maid used a card key to open double doors leading into spacious living accommodations.

As they entered, Serena noted the walls of the suite were painted olive, contrasting nicely with the honey-colored furniture. A chocolate leather love seat and matching chair made for comfortable seating. Outside on a wooden deck were teak lounge chairs and a hot tub that might easily seat eight. A small garden with convincing fake flowers had a fountain guarded by a statue of Aphrodite.

The maid pointed to an area they hadn't entered yet.

"Your bedroom, ladies."

The room held twin beds and a gigantic console with a television, VCR and DVD player. A huge picture window let in sunlight and glimpses of blue water, as well as the mansions on the Fort Lauderdale waterfront.

Pia, as enthusiastic as ever, kicked off her high heels and plopped onto one of the beds.

"I might just get used to this," she enthused. "I can't wait to get out of this clothing. When will our luggage arrive?"

"Your bags are already here, madam."

The attendant threw open the double doors of the closet to show them where their luggage was stashed. "I can get the butler to help you unpack," she offered.

Both women exchanged looks. No butler, at least not right now. There were just some things a woman preferred to do on her own.

"We'll take care of our own unpacking but we'd like help with ironing our dresses later," Serena said, speaking for both of them.

"As you wish. If you do not need anything else, I will leave you ladies to relax."

Bowing, the attendant backed out of the room.

When she was gone, Serena poured two glasses of champagne from the bottle chilling in the ice bucket. Next to it was a large gift basket. She handed Pia her wine.

"To a much needed vacation," she said, clinking her glass against her friend's.

Pia waved the embarkation brochure at Serena. "I'll drink to that. Let's hope there are some classy men aboard that we'll enjoy dancing with. Have you looked at the workshop and competitive dancing schedules? They're inserted in the brochure."

"Yes, just briefly. I can't believe we found this themed dance cruise. I've had this fantasy since I was a little girl about being a professional ballroom dancer. I love my publishing career, but the stress of deadlines is wearing me down."

Kicking off her shoes, Serena joined Pia on the bed.

"Being a psychiatrist is no picnic either, *querida*," her friend confided. "There are times I just have to bite my tongue. I'm paid to listen and not to judge."

"You're a wonderful doctor, Pia, and an incredible friend. We'll use these next two weeks to recharge our batteries."

"I'll definitely drink to that."

Serena poured more champagne. For the next half hour, the friends perused the workshop schedule, circling the names of dance instructors they wanted to take lessons from. Although Serena didn't think she was good enough to enter the competitive dancing heats, she was willing to give it a try.

The alcohol went down easily, making her relax. She'd been edgy and jet lagged from the long plane trip from Buenos Aires. "Did you see there's a treasure hunt as part of the cruise?" Pia asked, flipping over the brochure. "It's based on a legend about the moon goddess and her lover. Whoever finds the hidden pendant is supposed to be lucky in love. Now that's something we could both use."

Serena set down her glass. Love was something she was unwilling to engage in anymore.

"I was thinking that the story of the moon goddess

and this lowly shepherd might make a good young adult's book," she mused. "Maybe I should write it myself instead of assigning it."

"Why don't you? You've got fourteen days to do whatever you want, *querida*."

Selena, Serena's twin, had been a hopeless romantic and would have jumped all over the idea. Maybe Serena would dedicate the book to her twin sister's memory.

Still toying with that thought, she opened the brochure, found the insert, and quickly reread the legend. It was a charming story and had lots of possibilities. Serena headed up the young adult division of her parents' publishing house, so it would be easy to get a book published.

"I wouldn't mind the perks that come with finding the pendant," Serena said dreamily. "Massages, beauty treatments, invitations to the ship's bridge. It all sounds wonderful to me."

"Don't forget the romance bit," Pia reminded her. "We could both use a good man in our lives."

Carlos had been Pia's great love. They'd dated for several years, and were engaged. Then with no explanation he had changed his mind and called things off. Later Pia had found out he'd taken up with a young woman almost half his age, and had no problem marrying her.

Serena thought about her own romantic woes. Six months ago she'd had a two week fling, but nothing had come of that either. He'd chosen the coward's way out, disappearing without so much as an explanation. As a result she was starting to develop serious trust issues with men.

Pia clapped her hands.

"*Bastante!* I'm starving. There must be something to eat in that gift basket?"

The huge basket wrapped in cellophane and topped with a jaunty yellow bow sat on the coffee table. Serena poked a hole in the wrapping with a manicured nail. She removed oranges, a pineapple, and mangos and laid them on the dresser along with peanuts, wedges of cheese and crackers. At the very bottom of the basket she spotted a velvet pouch.

"What's this?" she said, swishing her wavy black hair off her face and balancing the pouch in the palm of one hand.

"Open it," Pia urged.

Alexandra's Dream listed slightly as Serena removed a silver teardrop pendant from the pouch and tossed it to Pia, who deftly caught it with one hand.

"*Caramba!* I think this is the treasure," Pia cried.

Simultaneously a male voice boomed over the intercom.

"Our mandatory lifeboat drill will commence in exactly ten minutes. All passengers are requested to make their way to their assigned muster stations."

Both women quickly found their life jackets and headed out.

"Take the pendant with you," Pia urged, giving Serena a little nudge and folding it into her hand. "We'll stop at the Guest Relations Desk after the drill and tell them the treasure has been found."

On the way downstairs, the women put on their life jackets and were directed to their muster stations. Forty five minutes later, after each passenger had been accounted for, and several tedious announcements made, the boat drill ended.

Braving a good-sized crowd on the stairwell, they made their way to the Guest Relations Desk and stood in line awaiting their turn. Finally, an attractive Indonesian purser with a name badge that read Kali looked up from her computer monitor.

"Can I help you?"

"You have a winner," Serena said, handing the velvet pouch to the woman.

"May I have your name and cabin number please?"

"Serena d'Andrea. I'm in a penthouse on Zeus." She patiently waited for further instructions.

Kali dangled the tear-shaped pendant from her index finger and called to some unseen person in a back room. "The treasure's been found." She handed Serena back the piece. "You're a winner, all right, but I don't think finding love on board will be a problem for you. There are quite a few hotties that are part of our Rhythm Dancers theme cruise."

"I guess we'll find that out at the Bon Voyage party," Pia interjected, "It should be starting any minute. Can you confirm where it is?"

A piece of paper that looked like a newspaper was slid across the counter at them. It listed all of the onboard events.

"Do you have the time now to be interviewed?" Kali asked. "I can get a photographer and video crew here if you do."

Serena shook her head and glanced at the clock on the back wall. "No way."

"Okay. We'll find you at the party. Whatever works best for you."

Back in the penthouse, after a quick shower, Serena slipped into a turquoise halter dress and began trying on different pieces of jewelry.

"What do you think of this necklace?" she asked Pia, holding up a string of irregularly shaped beads.

"I think you should wear the pendant," Pia urged. "Let's see if it lives up to its name." She handed Serena a polishing cloth. "Give it a good rub and it should brighten up."

Serena took the cloth from her and made a wry face. "Okay. It's bound to encourage conversation at least."

After polishing the piece, Serena removed the chain and threaded a satin ribbon through the loop and tied it around her neck. The silver pendant contrasted nicely with her tanned skin.

"Perfect," Pia announced. "You look like a moon goddess yourself."

"You're good for my ego. What would I ever do without you?"

"Live a full, happy life. Making people feel good about themselves is what I do for a living. If I can do it for patients, I most certainly can do it for my best friend."

Pia wiggled into a form-fitting sleeveless dress that only someone who weighed one hundred and eight pounds would dare to wear.

"How do I look?" she asked, placing one hand on her hip and posing.

"Stunning, you always do."

"Thank you. Now let's go to the party and see if we can find ourselves dance partners."

Linking arms, the two women headed out.

TRACY DOWNED another glass of Alka Seltzer and hoped her stomach would settle. In half an hour she had a dance rehearsal and she expected the phone to ring any moment. When it did, she wasted no time picking up.

"Hello," she said, breathlessly.

"It's Kali. I'm calling as promised. An Argentine woman found the pendant. Her name is Serena d'Andrea and she's in a penthouse suite. She's a babe, tall, stunning and has the most beautiful eyes. The men on this cruise will be tripping over their feet to dance with her."

"Has the video crew interviewed her yet?"

"No, she was in a hurry, so they'll do it at the Bon Voyage party in La Belle Epoque. Why are you so interested in this pendant anyway?"

"Call me a hopeless romantic."

"Aren't we all? Listen, I have to run. This Rhythm Dancers group is driving me crazy. They've taken over the ship and there's a very long line at the front desk."

After Kali hung up, Tracy paced the small cabin. Time was running out. She needed to get her hand on that pendant and soon. Sal had grown impatient and his threats that she would never see her baby boy again had increased. He'd managed to get hired on board as an escort. That sent a clear message that he thought she was a screw up.

With some trepidation Tracy punched in Sal's number and waited for him to pick up. What a con artist he was. He'd certainly sold her a bill of goods. When they were dating he'd told her what she'd wanted to hear, and she'd married him convinced that he would take care of her. But once the ring was on her finger, he'd turned into a woman's worst nightmare. He became abusive.

In a matter of time she found out that Sal Morena was no more than a small time hood. He needed the attention of women to keep his ego fed, and he enjoyed manipulating them and seeing their reactions. It was all about Sal—no one else mattered. How he'd managed to talk his way into a job as a dance escort was anyone's guess. The man was no Fred Astaire.

Tracy's anxiety built as the phone continued to ring. She was about to hang up when Sal's gruff voice finally came on the line.

"Prego!"

"Sal, it's Tracy."

"What's taken you so long to get back to me?"

"I was waiting for my friend at the Guest Relations desk to call. An Argentinean woman by the name of

Serena d'Andrea found the pendant. She's in a suite on Zeus. She's a member of the Rhythm Dancers group and she'll be attending the Bon Voyage party."

"Grazie," Sal snorted. "I'll be attending that party, too, and I'll be sure to become acquainted with the d'Andrea woman. I'll pretend to be interested in her, regardless of whether she's a dog or not." Another raucous laugh followed. "I'll just have to fantasize that she's a supermodel, and do whatever it takes to get my hands on that pendant."

What a pig he was. She must have been out of her mind to have slept with him, much less married the man.

"How is Franco, Sal? When will you give him back to me?"

An ugly snort followed, and another derisive chuckle.

"When you deliver on your promises, and I have that pendant in my hot little hands, then maybe you'll get your son back."

"But Sal that's not what we agreed…"

"But Sal, nothing. You've had ample opportunity to get me that pendant, and you've botched each and every attempt. That weasel Giorgio managed to get himself arrested without paying my gambling debt. Now that pendant is mine. Excuse me. I must go and get ready for the party."

"And I have dance rehearsal," Tracy said, smothering a sob.

She laid the receiver down and swiped at her eye. What more did Sal expect of her? She was feeding him information as soon as she got it. And in exchange he had promised to give her back her son. *Their* son, though you would never guess it from his actions.

Her child was the one person who loved her unconditionally. She would do just about anything to hold him in her arms again.

She had to help Sal get that pendant. She had to.

CHAPTER TWO

ON BACCHUS DECK, the five hundred plus passengers who'd signed up for the Rhythm Dancers charter were packed into La Belle Epoque. When Serena and Pia entered the dance club, people were milling around the champagne bar sipping colorful drinks.

The information in the pamphlet indicated that the group was a diverse one, coming from different dance clubs around the world. Many passengers had signed up for the chance to rub shoulders with the pros and take lessons from the best. The more confident dancers were already out on the floor executing complicated twist and turns. So much for noncompetitive dancing.

The Bon Voyage party had been touted as the ultimate ice breaker: an opportunity for dancers to mingle and get to know each other. From the looks of things, it was shaping up to be a very competitive event, with dancers using the occasion to showcase themselves. Since it was standing room only, Serena and Pia found a spot off to the side with a decent view of the floor.

"I'm going to have to try my best not to analyze

some of these people,' Pia said, "I'll get us drinks. If you're not here when I get back I'll find you." With that she hurried off.

Serena was left to people watch. She'd come aboard hoping to find a dance partner, someone who was looking to have fun with no strings attached. She was determined the next fourteen days were going to be divided between writing and working on her rhythm dancing. She owed it to her twin, Selena, to write that book, and she planned on following through.

Pia soon came hurrying back with a tall, fair-skinned ship's officer in tow. He carried their drinks.

"This is Andreas Zonis," she announced, gesturing to the officer to hand Serena her glass.

Serena accepted the drink and shook the man's hand. They exchanged the usual pleasantries, but Andreas, clearly interested in Pia, shifted his attention back to her friend.

Feeling like a third wheel, Serena cast another glance around the crowded room. Her eyes lingered on a tall, dark-haired man in pressed jeans, and a short-sleeved linen shirt tucked neatly in his pants. He had broad shoulders and a narrow waist. Serena's gaze traveled the length of him, stopping at his feet. He wore silver-tipped leather boots with a thick heel that added to his considerable height.

Painful memories came flooding back, so much so that she couldn't help giving him a second look. He was too far away to get a close-up of his face, but he reminded her of the man she'd met in Buenos Aires, the man who'd broken her heart.

With a concentrated effort she tried to focus on the here and now. It had been six months since she'd last laid eyes on Marc LeClair and she should be over him by now. But how did you forget a man who'd seemed perfect for you—a man who'd made you laugh so hard your sides ached. Marc, of the jet-black wavy hair, and to die-for blue eyes. She'd fallen hard and fast, and moving on wasn't easy.

Serena could still hear his raspy voice whispering endearments in her ear. When she closed her eyes, his unique spicy scent tickled her nostrils. With vivid clarity she remembered how he'd held her, loved her.

"Serena, you are a dream come true," he'd said. "The woman I've been waiting for."

Lines. All of it. And she'd bought them hook, line and sinker, convincing herself there was a future for them. She'd said those three little words *I love you.* Words she'd never said to another soul. And that was the beginning of the end, she suspected, because after that he'd disappeared.

The dark-haired man was laughing at something the woman next to him said. Serena wasn't close enough to hear him, but Marc's laughter had been distinctive and hardy, and this man certainly looked as if he was enjoying himself.

The resemblance was truly uncanny, although she'd never seen Marc dressed so casually or appear so relaxed. Marc LeClair had been polished and put together, and he'd said he had a twin. Serena wondered if this could be the twin brother.

His being a twin was another reason she'd been drawn to him. Twins had a special bond, an intuitive understanding of each other. She and Selena had been able to communicate without saying a word. And she and Marc shared a love of ballroom dancing and old movies, the kind where people wore elegant clothing and knew how to foxtrot.

In an especially intimate moment, Serena had shared with Marc the dark times after her sister's equestrian accident when she could not get out of bed. Serena had been depressed and one step away from ending it all. It had been a painful heartbreaking experience. If she hadn't had Pia to lean on she would probably not have made it through. It was Pia who'd been there to help her through that awful time after Marc dumped her, too.

"Dios mío!" Serena hissed, elbowing her friend in the gut and sloshing liquid from their glasses. "It is him."

"Him who?" Pia answered distractedly, her attention still focused on the handsome cruise ship officer.

The attractive redhead was now whispering something in the look-a-like Marc's ear. Her plunging neckline threatened to spill her considerable assets, and using those assets to her advantage, she brushed her breasts against the man's arm.

Serena couldn't help but gape. How could two people possibly look so much alike? On the one hand she hoped it wasn't him. He was the last person she wanted to run into on her vacation. She was still embarrassed and more than a little angry at the manner in which their brief relationship had ended. She'd followed her heart and given in to passion, ending up in his bed. He'd said he loved her, yet he'd left her without a word; not a note or a follow up phone call. He'd treated her like a pick-up and she couldn't easily get over that.

She was tempted to confront him just for the satisfaction of seeing him squirm. But what if it wasn't Marc? Serena wished she could discuss her options with Pia. But her psychiatrist friend was too busy flirting with the hot-looking officer. Later maybe, they would have one of their talks.

To take her mind off the man who reminded her so much of Marc, Serena gulped her rum punch and focused on the female members of the Rhythm Dancers group. The women wore everything from microminis and swirling ankle-length skirts to Daisy Dukes, those sexy low rise cut-offs that Argentine women would only be seen in if their bodies were perfect, but Americans wore confidently regardless of their size.

Serena smoothed the skirt of the turquoise sundress and glanced down to admire the silver three-inch heel sandals she'd thought were sexy. At five feet eight inches she hardly needed the additional height, but standing out in a crowd helped boost her confidence. She fingered the teardrop pendant and returned her attention to the dance floor.

Across the way, a tall, olive-complexioned man lifted his glass and winked at her. Simultaneously the ship's whistle blew and a voice boomed over the intercom.

"It is with great pleasure the crew of *Alexandra's Dream* welcomes The Rhythm Dancers. If you have not done so already, please make your way to deck six for your Bon Voyage party."

The dark skinned man continued to stare at her although she tried her best to ignore him. Something about him made her stomach churn and normally she did not have this strong a reaction to anyone. She kept her gaze on the dance floor, listening to the host and hostess, an Argentine and American pair. On a raised dais behind them, a D.J. adjusted the knobs of his stereo equipment, turning the volume up high. He was warming up the crowd already tapping their feet irritably.

More and more people began gravitating toward the dance floor. Pia was now trying to convince the officer to give it a whirl.

"I'm not a very good dancer," he said in a Greek accent. "You mentioned you've been taking lessons for years. I will make a fool of myself."

"No you won't," Pia insisted. "If you let me lead you, we can salsa like pros."

Serena bet they would do a lot more than salsa if Pia had her way. Pia was a smart, confident woman extremely comfortable in her sexuality, and not the least bit shy about going after what she wanted. Right now the handsome officer was at the top of her list.

Pia had chosen a profession well suited to her. She'd always been the insightful one, forever in tune with people's thoughts and motivations. If she hadn't been away at a symposium when Marc LeClair had come to town, maybe Serena's involvement with him would not have gone as far as it had.

Pia was now dragging the awed officer onto the dance floor, leaving Serena alone.

"Would you like to dance?" an accented male voice asked over her shoulder. The man who'd been gawking held out his hand. He was tall, tanned, and had spiky, gelled, black hair.

"Um, I'm waiting for my friend."

"She is dancing and you should be, too. My name is Salvatore Morena. My friends call me Sal." He pointed at her neck. "That's quite the pendant."

"Thank you. Serena d'Andrea," Serena said, accepting his hand because she had no choice.

For some unexplainable reason her instincts were telling her this was not a nice man.

Sal placed a hand lightly on Serena's shoulder blade as they began to salsa.

"Serena," he repeated, bringing her hand to his lips and kissing her palm. "*Bellissima.* Serena means the calm one. I am in the jewelry business and I know a nice piece when I see one." He reached as if to take the pendant in his hand.

Determined to avoid his touch, Serena stumbled. Sal brought her right back into step.

"Perhaps some time during this cruise you will allow me to appraise the piece?"

She didn't respond right away, and Sal wondered if maybe he was losing his touch. He was a good-looking man, he'd been told, earthy, without an excess ounce of fat on him. Most women would have been eating up the flattery and been all over him by now.

Time to turn up the wattage a notch.

Sal directed his most melting gaze at Serena. She didn't seem particularly impressed. Usually women got excited when they heard he was in the jewelry business. Immediately visions of diamonds began dancing in their heads.

"What do you say, Serena, will you entrust your pendant to me so I can appraise it?"

"Uh...perhaps," she answered, making it sound as if he wasn't exactly trustworthy. "But it's not really mine."

All too soon the lively salsa came to an end and another began. Sal tightened his hold on her before she could run off. If she knew how turned on he was maybe she'd loosen up a bit.

"Why are you in such a hurry, *bella?* The evening is young and I'm enjoying dancing with you," he whispered in her ear.

Serena muttered something he didn't quite hear and continued to dance. She was a good dancer and used her hips seductively. It wasn't a hardship holding her close, since she was curvy in all the right places. If things went as planned, he wouldn't have to fake interest in her.

Someone tapped him lightly on the shoulder. Sal swung around, his infamous glare in place. Damn. The man had a camcorder in his hand. He must want to film Serena.

Sal was reluctant to turn her over to the man, especially when he was just warming her up. By the time he was through making love to her, she'd be begging him to take that pendant from between her beautiful olive breasts. He just needed to work on getting her to trust him.

"Is there something you wanted?" Sal asked the cruise ship employee.

"Yes, we'd like to interview the person who found the pendant."

Sal spotted another videographer lurking in the background. On second thought this might well be the time to make himself scarce. He couldn't risk having his mug plastered on every in-cabin television or the videos passengers bought to take home. He'd be the first person they came after when that pendant went missing.

SERENA'S PRAYERS HAD been answered. She'd been saved, and not a minute too soon. She'd come this close to kneeing her dance partner in the groin. Granted, she wasn't crazy about being interviewed by the video staff, but anything was better than having this man rubbing up against her while pretending to dance.

"Where would you like to conduct your interview?" she asked the man with the camcorder.

"Here on the dance floor," he said, sticking a microphone under her nose. "You're with the Rhythm Dancers group so that means you much prefer fast dancing to slow."

"*Sí*. Yes, I am and yes I do."

"Your native language is Spanish but you speak English perfectly. Where are you from?"

"Argentina."

"Cool!"

Serena, conscious of the camcorder whirring away, looked around frantically for Pia. Her friend handled the spotlight much better than she did.

Pia had found herself another dance partner, so Serena knew she was on her own. She fingered the pendant around her neck and stared into the lens of the camera.

Her interviewer had a serious expression on his face as he held the microphone, and spoke into it in exaggerated tones.

"Once upon a time, according to Greek mythology, a moon goddess dared to fall in love with a commoner, a humble shepherd no less. This very much angered her suitor, the god Zeus, no less. In his jealousy Zeus killed the shepherd. The devastated moon goddess wept and wept until her tears threatened to flood the earth. Finally she was convinced to stop. One of those teardrops fell on the beautiful diamond clasp of the cloak that concealed the two lovers, hiding it forever. To this day, silver teardrop pendants are a sign of true love, and the person who finds our shipboard pendant is guaranteed to be lucky in love."

His companion stepped forward, taking over.

"Will Serena d'Andrea be lucky enough to find a shipboard romance? Let's hear what she has to say."

The microphone was thrust under Serena's nose again.

"How does it feel to have discovered the pendant?" the crew member asked.

Serena, conscious of every eye on her, smiled into the camera. Even the people who'd been dancing had stopped.

"It was a big surprise. There it was right at the bottom of the gift basket. I certainly didn't expect to find it."

"Are you excited about the prospect of wearing the pendant around the ship and maybe finding your own true love?"

The camera zoomed in to capture the pendant nestled between Serena's cleavage.

Caught off guard by the directness of the question, Serena fingered the piece. "Searching for the pendant was fun, and I enjoyed reading the story of the shepherd Lexus and his love for the moon goddess. I'd like to believe that some day I will find my true love."

"Do you believe true love exists?" the other videographer asked, stepping forward.

Of course she believed in love. But love hurt and could be painful if unrequited. She'd learned that the hard way by falling for Marc LeClair, the man who'd broken her heart.

Serena glanced in the direction where she'd last seen the man she'd thought might be Marc Le Clair. He was no longer there and neither was the redhead.

"My friend is a very romantic woman," Pia said,

coming up beside her. "She is excited about the possibility of meeting Señor Right aboard *Alexandra's Dream.* Aren't you, *querida?*" Pia placed an arm around Serena's shoulders and smiled for the camera.

Caught up in her friend's enthusiasm, and buoyed by her support, Serena managed another bright smile. She held the pendant between her thumb and forefinger, making sure the camera crew got a good shot of the piece.

"Of course. Let's hope this brings me good luck."

Applause broke out around her. The disk jockey cranked up the music louder, signaling the interview was officially over. Dancing immediately resumed.

But the music was quickly cut off when a commanding voice called over the intercom, "We have officially set sail for Hemingway's Key West. We wish you a safe and enjoyable journey. Bon voyage!"

CHAPTER THREE

"YOU DANCE LIKE A NATIVE," the redhead said coyly. She'd commandeered Marc's arm and practically dragged him onto the dance floor. With each sultry move her oversized breasts grazed his chest, but he still didn't know her name, nor was he particularly interested in finding out.

"You could say I am a native," Marc answered smoothly, executing an underarm turn. "My mother was Argentinean, so I learned to dance practically before I could walk."

"Argentinean." She looked at him, awed. "I thought you were a good ole boy from Texas. I checked out your boots."

He wasn't sure how to take that. Was it a come on?

"I'm from Canada. Alberta's where I was born, but I've been working in Texas for a couple of years. The boots are my tribute to Texas, but we've got lots of cowboys in Alberta, too."

"Cool!"

Marc couldn't wait for the dance to end. He had no desire to discuss his personal life with a stranger. He tried taking the lead since he could almost hear her counting the salsa beat in her head, but she wouldn't let him.

Quick, quick, slow. Quick, quick, slow. Although not exactly proficient in salsa, she faked it, using a lot of hip and breast movement to make it look authentic.

"I'm Heddy," she said, her lips close to his ear.

"Heddy? That's an unusual name."

"It's actually Heather Maxwell but I hate Heather."

"Heather's a beautiful name," Marc murmured.

From the moment he'd arrived at the party, she'd attached herself to him. She'd even accompanied him to the Guest Relations Desk to straighten out a problem with his onboard charge card when his purchase didn't go through. She seemed pleasant enough but not terribly bright. Right now she was providing a welcome distraction, helping him get his mind off the real reason he'd been forced to take this sudden vacation.

A hand tapped his shoulder. He jumped. He was still jittery and on edge, and rightly so, given everything he'd been through.

"May I cut in?" a well-groomed, dark-haired man asked. He eyed Heddy.

"Of course."

Ignoring Heddy's frantic headshakes, Marc quickly turned her over to the man and left the dance floor.

As he made his way across the room, Marc noticed a group of people gathered around someone. His first thought was that it must be one of the celebrity instructors putting on a solo performance. Curious, he slowed his pace, hoping to see one of the greats, but as bits of conversation floated his way, he realized he'd been mistaken.

"It must feel great finding the pendant," a woman's high-pitched voice shrilled. "You're bound to get lots of attention."

"With looks like that, you don't need a pendant," another voice called out. "Hand it over, girl. Some of us need it more."

"Did the cruise staff tell you what kinds of perks you'll get if they find you wearing the pendant?"

Marc couldn't hear the responses to the questions but guessed the fuss had something to do with the treasure hunt mentioned in the embarkation pamphlet. He'd passed on hunting for the pendant. Finding love wasn't in the cards right now; his primary focus was staying alive.

He was on this ship for two reasons—first, because he'd been ordered by his boss to disappear, and second, because there was nothing he enjoyed more than dancing. Dancing was a great stress reliever. And for the next fourteen days he could take lessons with the best.

There had been threats on his life recently, followed by a dozen or so near mishaps. Marc was ordered to take a vacation and forced out of his beloved Colombia. Leaving the country he loved and his high-profile position at the Canadian embassy only added to his stress, but at least the dance-themed cruise would keep him from thinking about it for a while.

He'd grown up taking dance lessons. Both of his parents had been accomplished dancers. High level government officials, they'd expected their children to know how to dance, and their social life revolved around various ballroom events. His mother, a South American socialite, and his father, also from a socially prominent Canadian family, thought it would instill confidence and at the same time keep them occupied.

At first, Marc had been resentful about having to go to dance classes when his friends were out playing sports. But as he got older he began to appreciate having this skill. Dancing had made adolescence far less painful. While his schoolmates had difficulty crossing a room to ask a girl to dance, he found it easy. And once he was on the floor he became another person, totally uninhibited. This made him a popular and sought-after date.

He stood now at the fringe of the crowd, curious to see who the crew members were filming. Whoever it was must be enjoying their fifteen minutes of fame and eating up the attention.

He caught a glimpse of turquoise clothing and wavy black hair and knew it was a woman. She must be hot since there was a disproportionate number of men in the crowd.

The music in the background swelled, and a female voice took over the microphone. The interview was over.

"It's lady's choice. Gals, it's your turn to grab yourself a man."

A stampede ensued as women pulled visibly reluctant partners onto the dance floor. Marc wanted to see the woman in the turquoise dress so he hung back. When she turned around and he saw her face, he stared. It couldn't be, but the flicker of recognition in those violet eyes told him it was Serena. No one had eyes quite like hers. He was transported back to another time, another place.

They were in a dance club, elegant and imposing, with winding staircases and a polished oak floor. He'd been taken there by a business colleague and his wife, people who weren't serious dancers but just out to have a good time. When Marc had spotted Serena on that dance floor, he'd known that *she* was the one.

He'd positioned himself in such a way that when the dance ended, he was in her path. He'd asked her to join him in a Viennese waltz, and one dance had led to another. They fell in step easily. The perfect fit. Quickly, too quickly, the evening had passed.

A look of revulsion now replaced the startled expression in Serena's eyes and she was staring at him as if he were some kind of rodent.

Marc had learned to school his expressions and keep his emotions under wraps. In his business you had to. He'd hoped and prayed for months that Serena d'Andrea would get in touch with him, and when that hadn't happened, he'd become resigned to never seeing her again. The irony of it was that she was now aboard this cruise ship with him. And he couldn't do a damn thing about it. He would not endanger her life.

Marc nodded, acknowledging her.

Serena's violet eyes traveled the length of him, but she maintained a respectable distance. At last she spoke.

"It's been a long time."

"Do we know each other?" The lie rolled easily off his tongue.

Serena's lips quivered slightly. She was thrown.

"Marc LeClair?" she asked, uncertainly.

"Sorry. I'm flattered and wish I were him. My name is Gilles Anderson. You are?"

"Serena d'Andrea," she answered in the smoky voice he remembered.

She was so beautiful. He'd fallen hard and he still hadn't recovered. Marc gave Serena a slow, lazy smile. He tried not to let the memories take over. It had been six months since he'd last seen her but it felt like yesterday.

Serena's winged eyebrows came together. She fingered the silver pendant and carefully looked him over.

"Gilles, were you in Buenos Aires about six months ago?"

He shook his head slowly. "I'm afraid not. I've been on business in Dallas, Texas, for the last year or so."

"What about Colombia then? Did you live there?"

Another slow shake of his head signaled his

puzzlement. "Can't say I have, though it's on my list of places to travel. Maybe after I get back home to Canada and tend to some business, I'll be ready to set off again."

"It's nice to meet you...Gilles," Serena said extending a hand. Her voice was heavy with skepticism. "How about we dance and get acquainted?"

He didn't know where this was going, but no way was he getting on a dance floor with her—at least not for a sexy Latin salsa—without blowing his cover. They'd spent two weeks in Buenos Aires getting as close as any two people could. They'd danced and alternately made love, sometimes doing both simultaneously. Serena knew all of his moves.

"I'm going to have to pass, I'm afraid. Besides I'm hopeless when it comes to rhythm dancing."

"I'll take the lead," she offered, coming right at him, her arms open.

"If he doesn't want to dance, I'd be happy to," a male voice said behind them. Without waiting for an answer, the man took Serena's hands and began tugging her onto the floor. She didn't look particularly happy but she went.

It had been a close call. The woman Marc had dreamed of and fantasized about for months, the woman who haunted his memories was here. Talk about poor timing.

The redhead was back.

"There you are," she said. "I've been looking everywhere for you." She held out a freshly made drink, which he took from her.

"Thanks."

"How come you're not dancing?" she asked, swiveling her hips. "I would have thought you could have any woman you want. You're the hottest guy on this ship."

Marc took a swallow of the clear-colored liquid. "What is this?"

"Rum and coconut water. The bartender's from the islands. I told him to make us one of his favorite local drinks."

Us? She was moving too fast for him, but she just might be what he needed to take his mind off Serena.

"We should dance," Heddy said, coming even closer, her gigantic breasts almost nudging his chest.

"Okay, how about when the music changes and things slow down."

"Perfect."

There was a wide smile on her face now. From his answer she probably figured he was interested in her. Marc felt a twinge of guilt.

After a few more songs the music changed and several enterprising couples began to cha-cha-cha. Setting down his almost empty glass, Marc gestured for her to do the same. Heddy carried her glass with her and they began a one handed cha-cha-cha.

They'd been dancing for several minutes when a shrill scream tore through the music. People began scattering.

"Stop him," a high pitched female voice shouted.

"Stop that thief. He tried to mug that woman."

"Oh, my God he was choking her."

A man plowed through the crowd, shoving people aside. He was heading directly toward them. Marc grabbed the half-filled glass that Heddy still held and flung the liquid into the man's face. He stumbled and went down like a brick, arms splaying to brace his fall. The object he held hit the floor and began to roll.

Marc straddled the man, grabbed one of his arms and twisted it behind his back, almost wrenching it from its socket.

"What the hell is wrong with you?" he snapped, applying pressure to the arm.

"Please, please, don't hurt me," the man whined. "I didn't steal anything."

Two passengers helped Marc keep the thief prone, until men wearing polo shirts with the *Alexandra's Dream* logo took over.

"Security," they barked, identifying themselves.

A pair of corded arms physically loosened Marc's grip. He was breathing hard from the exertion of keeping the thief still.

The security man's buddy placed a gigantic boot-clad foot on the small of the man's back.

"You were great," a woman in an elaborate ball gown gushed, her hand grazing Marc's forearm. "What if he'd had a weapon?"

"Way to go, bud," another man said.

Marc was still dazed, unable to believe that something like this could happen on a cruise ship. People were gawking, shocked, watching the thief as he was pulled to his feet and cuffed.

A man in ship's whites, a stethoscope draped around his neck, pushed through the crowd. He was escorted by another security type. They headed for a woman seated in a lounge chair and surrounded by cruise personnel who were holding passengers back from the area.

Serena! Marc's heart pounded in his chest. Was she all right? There would be hell to pay if she was hurt. A woman squatting next to her held her hand, offering water periodically. A crew member held a cold compress to the side of her neck and a tall, broad shouldered man who looked to be in charge had an anxious look on his face.

It must have been her jewelry the thief was after. He'd ripped the necklace off without caring whether he hurt Serena or not. Marc should have broken the bastard's arm. He swallowed the bile that was slowly rising in his throat and fought to get his emotions under control.

The doctor removed the compress, revealing an ugly bruise on Serena's neck. As the medic's fingers probed the area, a man with a hip-rolling walk approached one of the security officers, muttering something in his ear. He was allowed access to the injured woman. He squatted down and folded something into her palm.

Serena opened her hand and brought the item closer to her. It shone under the artificial lighting, just like the tears in her eyes.

If Marc ever got hold of that bastard, the guy would live to regret what he'd done. Only a coward would hurt a woman.

CHAPTER FOUR

THANASI KALDIS, the hotel director, ran a tanned hand through hair that was beginning to silver at the tips. He ground his teeth in frustration. This contract had been nothing but a nightmare from the very start. He'd been stuck with a mostly North American crew who weren't used to working long hours, and complained every chance they got. And he'd had passenger issues on every single cruise. Retirement was beginning to sound better and better.

What had happened to the days when people came on board a cruise to eat, drink and relax? Now there was always an agenda or some kind of incident that required the police or law enforcement.

He had been happy to leave the Mediterranean, figuring all the drama of the onboard smuggling scheme that had been uncovered was over with. In the Caribbean he was hoping to get back to some kind of normalcy. But no, Patti Kennedy, his cruise director, and the ship's librarian had come up with this ridiculous treasure hunt. Now, even before the ship sailed, passengers were frantically going through their cabins and moving furniture around.

He was counting the days to vacation. At the end of this cruise, when the ship repositioned and sailed down the west coast of South America, Thanasi was taking a much needed break. After attending Ariana Bennett's wedding, it was off to Athens to see his family.

Ariana was the ship's librarian and she was marrying a former undercover Italian police officer, Dante Colangelo, who'd been investigating the smuggling ring. He'd abducted her at a dig site, suspecting she was involved in the antiquities black market. But after spending time together and discovering that neither was the enemy, the two had fallen for each other. They'd planned a shipboard ceremony so that all Ariana's cruise staff friends could be there; the more elaborate wedding and reception would be held in Ariana's hometown, Philadelphia.

During his vacation, Thanasi was going to seriously consider getting a job shoreside. He'd been toying with the idea for a while, especially after the smuggling scandal, but usually dismissed it because wanderlust got in the way. But even these past few voyages had not been incident free, and a nice dull desk job on shore was sounding better and better.

Thanasi was especially upset by this most recent attack. Alarm bells were bound to sound off to the media. The d'Andrea woman was an heiress from a prominent Buenos Aires family. Since past sailings had ended with arrests, Thanasi was dreading contacting the authorities again.

It would mean another delay and the inevitable

itinerary adjustments. The result would be passengers complaining. And if the d'Andrea woman decided to press charges, well, that would create even more problems and a longer delay.

Thanasi hated dealing with the authorities at foreign ports of call, but maritime law being what it was, he had no choice. Luckily they were in Key West. Still, it would mean kissing off his cherished personal time. He would now be too busy with the police and FBI.

Thanasi and Nick Pappas, the captain, would have to be available for questions. Nick had already placed a call to the owner, Elias Stamos, who was at his vacation home in Barbados. Elias should be calling back any minute.

Meanwhile the assailant had been taken to the brig, an isolated cabin kept open to contain unruly passengers. Now it was left to Thanasi and Patti Kennedy to get things back on track and deliver the cruise experience these passengers had come onboard for.

Patti, resilient and perky as ever, was already on the dais and in full command of the microphone while the Rhythm Dancers D.J. sat silently, headphones on, gaping at her. She was keeping things upbeat and light, trying to play down the seriousness of the situation yet at the same time not trivializing the attack. He had to admit she was good at her job.

Initially Thanasi had had his doubts about Patti. He was more comfortable working with male cruise directors. But although Patti's style was different, she'd delivered to date. She was pleasant, outgoing, humorous and a very attractive woman, especially popular with male passengers, who came up with outrageous excuses to interact with her.

"Well, now that we've had our entertainment for the evening," Patti announced, smiling her big smile, and tossing a full mane of chestnut hair off her face, "we can get ahead with the business of enjoying this cruise. Be assured the thief is under lock and key, in a cabin far away from you and me, thank goodness." She gave a throaty laugh and the passengers laughed with her.

"It's safe to return to your cabins to get ready for dinner. First seating will be in exactly half an hour. If you prefer alternative dining, then the Marco Polo and Olive Grove are the places to be. Both restaurants serve until eleven. And after dinner you'll love one of our Las Vegas style shows. The entertainment features our talented dancers, the *Alexandra's Dream* Team. Thanasi Kaldis, your hotel director, and I will be out on the Promenade later to answer your questions."

Patti surrendered the microphone to the clearly smitten D.J., who helped her down from the dais. She was immediately surrounded by people. Hoping to take the pressure off her, Thanasi made his way over.

Seconds before he got to the stage, a tall, dark-haired man in expensive boots accosted him. "You're the hotel director, aren't you?"

"I am." Thanasi held out his hand. "Thanasi Kaldis at your service." The passenger grasped it with a surprising firmness that almost made him wince. Thanasi quickly stuck his hand in the pocket of his navy blue double-breasted jacket and waited to hear what he would say.

"The name is Gilles Anderson," he said. "How could something like this happen on a cruise ship? That woman could have been seriously hurt."

Thanasi had asked himself the very same question, except he'd phrased it differently. How could something like this *continue* to happen on his cruise ship?

He was used to people drinking too much and occasionally causing a scene. He was used to couples fighting, the occasional extramarital affair gone awry, one-night stands that turned into a disaster when one or another party expected more, the disappearance of items from cabins, people complaining about food. But smuggling and passengers attacks were different from the usual experience. And this public assault of a passenger on his ship was definitely not to be tolerated.

"It's an unfortunate situation," Thanasi answered, keeping his voice modulated and his response professional. "This ship holds a thousand passengers and is very much like a floating city. We have metal detectors that passengers pass through prior to boarding, and the luggage goes through a scanner. Short of running background checks on all of our guests, we are doing our best."

Gilles Anderson didn't appear appeased by his answer. In fact he'd become more indignant. His face had taken on a crimson undertone, and Thanasi could tell he was fighting to control his anger.

"Where was your security force when that woman was attacked? Have you seen the ugly bruise on her neck? You'll be lucky if she doesn't sue you."

Thanasi had thought about that too. Americans were a litigious group, although Ms. d'Andrea was Argentinean. The first thing he'd had the Guest Relations personnel do was check her travel documents and that's how he'd discovered who she was.

"I repeat, it was a very unfortunate situation and we'll do everything in our power to make Ms. d'Andrea's stay with us as comfortable as possible." Thanasi removed his hand from his pocket and tried to discreetly pass on some beverage coupons to the Anderson man. "Please try to put this ugly situation behind you and allow me to buy you a drink or two."

The man recoiled as if he had been struck.

"Don't try to mollify me. I don't want complimentary drinks. I just want to be assured that none of us will have to worry about our safety on board."

Thanasi nodded. "I understand. As stated, this was a highly unusual situation. I've already alerted the authorities and we're putting steps in place to increase security." He turned, hoping the videographers were still shooting. Spotting them, he said, "See over there? Every movement's been recorded on film. It was stupid of that man to try stealing the pendant, because as soon as we look at that tape he's as good as caught. You have my assurance security will be visible for the rest of the cruise, and if necessary we'll have headquarters fly back-up personnel in."

Patti walked over to join him.

"Hi, I'm Patti Kennedy, your cruise director. Is there something I can help with?"

Gilles Anderson turned and immediately his stance became less aggressive.

"We have it all sorted out, I think. Nice job you did soothing the fears of the passengers and reminding us what we're here for." He smiled at Patti, seeming to like what he saw.

Patti flashed the man another wide smile, one that revealed perfectly straight white teeth and made her tanned skin look even darker. She was one of those people who came across as happy, healthy and even-keeled under the most adverse circumstances.

"Thank you. You're very kind," she said. "Why don't you stop by the Emperor's Club later and join Thanasi and me for grappa."

Thanasi felt a flicker of annoyance as he watched the flirtatious exchange, but at least he had been included in the invitation. He just hoped he wouldn't turn out to be the third wheel or the chaperone.

"Sounds good to me—I'll be there," Gilles said, smiling back and looking at Patti as if she'd just told him he'd won another cruise. Patti could charm the most disgruntled passenger.

"Look, I'm sorry about giving you a hard time," Gilles said, turning back to Thanasi. "I'm just concerned about what happened to that woman. I came to relax and I don't want to have to keep looking over my shoulder."

Thanasi touched the man's forearm lightly. "Not

a problem. I understand. Trust me, your safety is my biggest priority. I'll see you at the Emperor's Club after the late show, then."

"I'll be there."

After Gilles Anderson left, Thanasi and Patti headed back to their offices. It seemed every step they took, they were stopped by anxious passengers who wanted to have their fears assuaged.

"You were very good with the Anderson man," Thanasi admitted grudgingly.

So far Patti had proven to be competent and supportive, but he'd never told her so. The two had completely different styles of dealing with people. She was more relaxed, looser, while he preferred a formal businesslike approach. It was what he was comfortable with and the way he'd been trained.

Patti tossed another devastating smile his way, the kind that went directly to a man's heart. "I guess I'm putting my 'charm school' training to good use, eh?"

She'd picked up the *eh* from the Canadian crewmembers, and while her words were said in jest, there was an underlying edge to them. Thanasi had been very vocal about letting the crew know that he wasn't a proponent of "charm school." Hospitality training taught the basics, but he truly believed the only way to know what it took to work a cruise ship and deal with people was to be hands-on. He'd had to learn from the bottom up and he felt that was an asset.

"Do you have time for a coffee?" he surprised himself by asking Patti.

For a fleeting moment her gold-flecked eyes registered shock, though she quickly recovered. She shot him another of those wide smiles. "Sure. Where would you like to go?"

"My office. We'll be able to talk without interruption."

Thanasi would have much preferred an alcoholic drink, but they were still on duty and both needed to keep a clear head. In an hour or so he'd be accompanying Sean Brady, the Acting Chief of Security, to the brig, where they would interrogate the thief and attempt to get a written confession from him.

Opening the door to his office, he stood aside to let Patti enter.

Her wide gaze swept the room before she eased into the chair he gestured her to. "You're always so organized and so neat," she said, taking the seat facing his desk. "I'm the total opposite."

"You just have your own style."

Thanasi had seen her office and could vouch that she wasn't a minimalist. Paperwork was piled in neat stacks, but she had mementos of her visits to different countries all over the place. Patti had everything from Love Leaves purchased in Grenada to Evil Eye trinkets collected in Istanbul. Her office reflected her personality. It was warm, friendly and a little bit over the top.

He, on the other hand, prided himself on order. The only way to keep on top of the arduous paperwork that came with his job was to have folders for everything. With the exception of his computer, the surface of his desk was clutter-free.

He picked up the phone and spoke into it.

"I need a fresh pot of coffee and Danish sent up right away."

"Danish," Patti murmured. "I'm not sure I can afford the calories."

"You don't need to watch your figure," Thanasi said bluntly, and watched two little red dots pop out on Patti's cheeks.

He'd never seen her blush before. She had a figure most women would kill for. He'd seen her in a swimsuit at the crew gym when she was swimming laps. She had a flat stomach, shapely breasts and long legs. She was the kind of woman men fantasized about but seldom could get.

"You flatter me," Patti said, smoothing her hands over hips that were almost nonexistent. "If I get too complacent the pounds start piling on. It's easy to let yourself go on a cruise ship with all this food around."

"Tell me about it."

Thanasi sucked in his gut, not that there was much there to suck in. During his off time, what precious little there was of it, he frequented the crew gym, pumping iron like a mad man. When you were forty-something you had to work at keeping in shape and keeping your stress-level down.

"Oops! There goes my beeper," Patti said, standing. "Rain check on that coffee. We'll catch up at the Emperor's Club later."

"What about dinner?"

Patti was halfway out the door. The consummate professional, she was already answering the call.

"ARE YOU SURE you're up to going to the dining room?" Pia asked as she watched Serena painstakingly layer foundation on her neck.

"Of course. I'm not going to let something as silly as a nasty bruise stop me from getting out and about." Serena continued smoothing makeup over the ugly black and blue bruise resulting from the attack. "Help me pick out something to wear to dinner and afterwards we'll take in a show."

Pia crossed over to the closet and threw the doors open. "I find it odd that you were the one singled out. There are a thousand people on board."

"It doesn't make a whole lot of sense to me either. A man kept bumping into me while I was dancing. All of a sudden there was this tug, and I was dragged across the floor. Thankfully the ribbon holding the pendant broke."

Pia sifted through the clothing the butler had ironed and hung in the closet. "And be thankful that passenger flung his drink in the thief's face or he might have escaped."

"What passenger?"

"The dark-haired guy wearing cowboy boots. The videographers were filming, and I saw the whole thing on the big screen T.V. That's how I knew." Pia handed an elegant silk pantsuit to Serena. "Try this. A lace camisole underneath and you're set. I'd wear the pendant, too—it would look good with black. No point in leaving it lying around the room after what happened. I can't imagine why anyone would try to steal it, though."

"I'll put it in my purse. My neck still aches." Serena popped the jewelry into her evening bag. She was still shaken up, and more terrified than she was willing to admit. All she wanted to do was put the unpleasant incident behind her. "I thought about handing it in, but I hate to let that man win. Besides, he was caught, so maybe the pendant does have some lucky charm."

Pia stood in front of the full-length mirror, finger-combing her hair, and putting the final touches on her makeup.

"This dark haired man, the one who threw the drink, what did he look like?" Serena asked.

"He was hot, sort of a Hugh Jackman type—you know, the Australian actor."

Serena bit down on her bottom lip.

"And this Jackman look-a-like is one of our dance group?"

"He might be. He was on the dance floor several times with that hot-to-trot redhead. I remember looking at him and thinking, *Now, there is one classy man.* He's got a golden tan, dreamy blue eyes, and a smile that could stop a woman's heartbeat." Pia must have noticed Serena's stricken expression. "*Dios Mío,* Serena, he's not the man you think is Marc?"

Serena nodded her head slowly. "He sounds like the passenger I pointed out to you earlier."

"Then you must contact him and thank him for his help."

"I suppose I could. If I speak with him at length I might be able to determine if he's really Marc in disguise."

"Have the maître d' send him a bottle of wine or something. He's bound to call you and thank you."

"Good idea. And while I'm at it, I'll also send a bottle of wine to the man who returned the pendant. Let's go. We'll be late for the second seating."

Serena picked up her purse and Pia followed her out. They'd both agreed that the Empire Room, the main dining room, would be their best choice for dinner. As they approached they spotted the long line of passengers waiting to enter.

"Why don't we come back in fifteen minutes after it opens," Pia suggested, "Now is as good a time as any to familiarize ourselves with the ship. If we start off on Helios we can work our way down."

Pia led the way to a glass elevator, and after a short wait they joined a number of people getting on. Among them was a chubby, middle-aged, overdressed woman, clutching the arm of a man in suit and tie. She poked Serena's arm and said, "Aren't you the woman that man attacked? I witnessed the whole thing."

"You did?"

"Yes. I told the security people that man was dancing way too close to you. All of a sudden he left his partner and lunged for your throat. We're from Kentucky. We don't have this kind of excitement at home."

"Well, at least he was caught," another passenger chimed in.

Everyone in the packed elevator was now staring at Serena. She was glad when the elevator stopped on Poseidon and several people got off.

"I hope he didn't hurt you too badly," the plump, plain-speaking woman said. The sentiment was echoed by several others and Serena thanked them for their kindness.

She was relieved when they reached Helios and she and Pia quickly circled the artificially lit sundeck.

"We'll need to spend some time here," she said as they did a quick walk-through of the Jasmine Spa, fitness center and Starlight Theatre. All the amenities of an upscale resort seemed to be here, the putting green, tennis courts, hot tubs and a spacious observation deck.

"Sign me up," Pia said enthusiastically.

"We'll come back tomorrow when it's light. Shall we take the stairs to the next deck?"

"Sure."

On deck eleven, Artemis, they stuck their heads into the main lounge aptly named the Court of Dreams. It was three stories high and very glitzy. It reminded Serena of a wedding palace with its ornate railings, sweeping staircases and marble steps.

In typical Renaissance style, cherubs floated on the clouds on the ceiling, and pink, white and gold upholstered sofas and chairs added to the dreamy effect. Tucked away in illuminated alcoves were vases of greenery and blooming roses or statues of the Greek gods and goddesses. On stage, angled slightly to the left, a massive, black concert grand piano dominated.

"This reminds me so much of a European grand concert hall," Pia exclaimed.

"It is rather elegant."

They took a quick look at the indoor and outdoor pools, popped into the Sunshine's American Diner, where families with kids were chomping on hamburgers and pizzas while enjoying a more casual dining experience.

"The Empire Room should be open by now," Serena suggested, heading for the stairs.

A tuxedo-clad maître d' and several assistants hovered at the entrance of the dining room, greeting the few people trickling in.

"May I seat you?" he asked. The women gave him their *Alexandra's Dream* cards. After scrutinizing them, he flashed an even larger smile. "I have been waiting for you."

Serena's eyebrows rose. "You have?"

"Yes, indeed. I will bring you to the captain's table. Please follow me."

CHAPTER FIVE

"NAME AND CABIN NUMBER, please." Sean Brady, Acting Chief of Security removed a notepad from his breast pocket.

The sullen man hugging the wall glared at him but kept his mouth shut. His arms were folded across his chest in a defiant gesture.

Thanasi was starting to get impatient. He had other things to attend to. If this stonewalling continued, he would be late for dinner and Nick would not be pleased.

Captain Nick Pappas had issued a command performance to join him at the Captain's Table, which meant there were VIPs on board who needed entertaining. Thanasi had become dependent on his hotel director and key officers to schmooze them.

"We can do this the easy way or the hard way," Thanasi interjected, slapping his palm against the brig's wall. "This is the high seas and there is no established protocol to follow. Either you tell us your name and cabin number or we'll go through your pockets and find out who you are ourselves. What will it be?"

The man gulped. A reaction at last. He was of slender build, and had a wild-eyed look as if he hadn't slept in a couple of days. Thanasi thought he might be one of the professional dancers.

"There were women on the dance floor wearing much more expensive jewelry. Why did you attack the woman with the pendant?"

"I did not attack anyone."

Words at last, and uttered in an accent Thanasi couldn't quite place.

"Then why were you running away?" Sean asked, making a note of the man's answers.

"I had to go to the bathroom."

"Before or after you ripped the pendant from the woman's neck? You were holding it when you tripped. It fell out of your hand." Sean continued to scribble.

"You can't prove a thing," the man said defiantly.

"Oh, yes we can. Name and cabin number, please."

Thanasi had finally had enough. "Look," he said, getting in between the two men. "Deny it all you want but we have you on film. Our video crew has everything recorded. You were seen snatching the necklace from the woman's neck and she has a very ugly bruise to prove it. We have you racing across the dance floor, and a clear view of the passenger throwing that drink in your face and you stumbling. We know you attempted to steal the pendant."

The man gave another visible gulp. Sean, who'd also grown impatient began patting down the man and going through his pockets.

"Aha, we have something here," he said, removing a billfold. He plucked out a credit card and said out loud, "Milutin Krupinsky. Now why would Milutin do something so stupid as to attack a woman in public? There are only so many places you can hide on a cruise ship."

Milutin's face settled into a defiant mask.

"What's your cabin number, Milutin?"

Thanasi was past playing games. He was now half an hour late for dinner and Nick Pappas would not be pleased. The commander was often short on people skills and depended on his officers to carry the conversation at his table. Good friends or not, Thanasi was sure to hear about his late arrival.

"I don't have one."

"If you're on board you have to have a cabin number."

Another stony glare.

"Let me put it to you this way," Thanasi said, getting into Krupinsky's face. "If you tell us what we need to know, we could make things a little easier for you when we turn you over to the authorities. If you don't, well—" he spread his hands wide "—who knows what could happen."

Still no answer, just the blink of an eye.

"Your documents indicate you're not an American citizen so you'd be sent home. I'm guessing the jails there aren't exactly comfortable hotels. You could be sleeping on the floor with vermin, maybe dining on bread and water. God forbid you get sick."

He was exaggerating, of course, but if the man

got scared, maybe that would loosen his tongue. His primary goal right now was to get Krupinsky to spill his guts.

"I do not want to go home," Milutin finally said, his eyes shifting back and forth. "I have rights. I will not say another word until I have a lawyer present."

Sean was close to losing his temper. "You've been watching too much television." He took a deep breath. "Maybe you don't understand. You are on the high seas and we're operating under maritime law. If you get taken off this ship and put in jail, your only hope might be your embassy."

This time Milutin visibly winced, and Thanasi moved in for the kill.

"So now that we've gotten that settled, were you acting alone?"

"Alone? I don't understand."

"Your English is perfect. Better than mine. Let me repeat this slowly. Do—you—have—an—accomplice—with—you?"

A stony silence prevailed, though the man's flinty eyes did a round robin again.

"Better speak up," Sean hissed, "or we'll leave you to the mercy of the authorities tomorrow."

Milutin's chin fell. He glared at them through hostile slits.

Enough already. No more pussyfooting with this man.

"Let Milutin mull things over for an hour or two," Thanasi suggested. "The police and the respective authorities will be on board tomorrow bright and early.

While he languishes in a jail in Key West, the paper-work might take weeks to process." Thanasi chucked Milutin under his chin. "I'll be back later."

As they prepared to leave, Milutin shouted, "I am a newly hired employee of yours—that should count for something?"

"Not if you're a thief."

Thanasi and Sean headed off in different directions.

Thanasi was hopeful that Patti had received the same invitation that he had. Nick liked having his key officers at the Captain's Table because it took pressure off him. He especially liked having those who were good with people and knew how to make his onboard guests feel welcome.

He was looking forward to watching Patti do what she did best—chat up guests and make them feel comfortable.

WINE WAS BEING POURED when Pia and Serena slid into vacant seats at the captain's table. They nodded to the occupants already sipping their drinks. Earlier they'd agreed that the only way to meet new people was not to appear joined at the hip. And they were all for meeting new people and finding dance partners.

"Our guests of honor are here," the raven-haired captain with the serious gray eyes said, raising his wineglass before slowly taking a sip.

Both women smiled in acknowledgment and

waited for their wine to be poured. Once that was done and Serena had her glass in hand, she looked at the people seated at her table. She was still shaken by the earlier incident, but she knew that no one would ever guess from her appearance.

To her right was a dark skinned, square-jawed man who looked vaguely familiar. He was the man who'd found the pendant. The seat to the left of her was empty. Pia sat on the other side of the table. And as wretched luck would have it, the man she thought might be Marc LeClair sat two chairs down from Pia. Tonight he was dressed in a dark suit, crisp white shirt and apricot tie. A lock of unruly dark hair flopped over one eye. A midnight-blue eye, as she recalled.

She had not been expecting him here. But he appeared completely unaware of her presence—or pretended to be. He spoke in low tones to one of the ship's officers.

Serena gulped her wine and set it down. She was beginning to feel flushed all over. Her gaze swept over the other members of the dinner party. There was a portly couple she'd never seen before, and the comfortable ease they shared spoke of a long association.

Two officers in dress whites flanked them; the male was Andreas, the man Pia had been chatting up, the other was the female cruise director. At the end of the table, a matron with hair sprayed into a stiff helmet and wearing every piece of flashy jewelry she owned was fawned over by Serena's dance partner, the man who'd introduced himself as Sal. The chair at the foot of the table remained empty.

Serena's attention now returned to the head of the table where the captain sat. He was engaged in conversation with a striking woman with exotic dark looks whose gold bracelets jangled with every movement. The beauty sat to his right, hanging on to his every word yet holding her own in the conversation. The seat to the commander's left was vacant.

Serena began slowly putting two and two together. The dinner party was an attempt to try to smooth over her frightening attack on the dance floor. Otherwise, why would she, Pia, Marc and the man who'd recovered her pendant be dining together at the captain's table? But how to explain Sal, the exotic looking woman, the staid couple, and the overdressed matron? Fill-ins, she decided.

Serena still didn't know the name of the man seated next to her, the one who'd found the necklace. She'd never thanked him properly and that was a shame. She took another sip of wine and gave him her most dazzling smile.

"I'm Serena d'Andrea," she said, holding out her hand. "We were not formally introduced. I really appreciate what you did, returning the pendant to me. Did you get the wine?"

"Yes, I did, and you are most welcome, *señorita*. You can repay me by saving me a dance or two. By the way, my name is Diego Montalban. I was born in the Dominican Republic but now I live in New York." He had the slightest accent. Diego glanced at her neck. "Why are you not wearing the necklace? It would go perfectly with your outfit."

Gay, Serena thought, and therefore safe. Diego liked to dance and spoke her native tongue, which made for a certain kinship, and if he could help her get rid of Sal, even better. Serena considered continuing the conversation in Spanish but felt it might be rude and uncomfortable for the others around.

"I do have a nasty bruise," she said, her finger absently stroking the side of her neck. "Right here aches like crazy, but I suppose I will live."

"I am sorry to hear that," Diego said. "Has the doctor prescribed a painkiller? People are loco these days. How could a *ladrón* possibly think he would get away with something so awful on a cruise ship?"

"Thieves get bolder and bolder," the older, heavy-set woman interjected in strident tones. She began to recount an episode that had happened to her in a foreign country almost a decade ago. The people around the table listened politely but did not interrupt.

A pair of blue eyes, the color of the ocean, flickered over Serena. There wasn't the slightest glimmer of recognition in their depths. Marc LeClair flashed a slow, lazy smile that turned Serena's insides out.

Somehow she managed to smile back. Had it not been for Marc, or whatever he was calling himself these days, the thief might have gotten away.

She was about to ask what kind of wine Marc drank when two of the ships' officers arrived.

"I'm sorry I'm late." Thanasi Kaldis, the hotel director said, sliding into the seat next to Serena. The other officer took the seat at the foot of the table.

"How are you feeling?" Thanasi asked, lowering his voice. "The doctor mentioned you refused his offer of painkillers."

Serena swirled her red wine and smiled at him. "I don't like pills. Hopefully, this excellent wine will help me to forget the entire episode."

"Well, you can be assured the thug is under lock and key, and two security guards are posted outside the brig."

"Do you know why he picked me? I can't imagine that pendant is of any value."

"We will find that out after the police question him."

Two waiters came over to take orders and the conversation was put on hold.

Pia, on the other side of the table, was conducting an animated conversation with Andreas. She'd forgotten Serena existed, and although Serena tried to catch her eye, Pia was too busy flirting to return the look. Only Marc LeClair seemed tuned in to the conversation.

Serena was beginning to feel as if she were starring in a B movie. She was certain that the man seated on the other side of the table was Marc LeClair, even if he was pretending to be someone else. At the far end, looking as if he'd like to inhale her, was Sal Morena. And Thanasi Kaldis, the very starched and buttoned down hotel director, had his arm around her chair.

The waiter returned and she gave him her order. When she looked up she caught Salvatore Morena's saucy wink.

He'd been perfectly pleasant so far, ingratiatingly so, but there was something about him that made her uneasy. Maybe it was the instant intimacy he'd tried to force down her throat. Or maybe it was simply that he was too smooth. Whatever, she made a mental note to avoid him at all cost.

When Serena broke eye contact her gaze locked with the cruise director's. Was that hostility she saw in those golden-brown orbs? Maybe she was mistaken, because Patti Kennedy was now smiling and speaking with the couple.

It was obvious the cruise director had a crush on her boss. Did Patti think she was the competition? Serena wondered if the woman's feelings were known to the hotel director.

The ship rolled slightly indicating they were moving.

"Are we finally out to sea?" she asked Thanasi.

"We have been for quite some time. The nice thing about a ship this size is the stabilizers. You barely feel movement."

"Who are the other guests here?" she asked.

Thanasi stood wineglass in hand, and whispered to her, "I will make introductions." More loudly he said, "I wish to propose a toast. May the dancers among us not break a leg." He chuckled at his bad joke. "And after we raise our glasses, we will go around and introduce ourselves."

Patti Kennedy joined him, holding up her glass. "To an enjoyable cruise. May the lovely Ms. d'Andrea find true love on board." The look she sent

Serena's way said otherwise. It shouted "Keep your mitts off my man." Serena hadn't been mistaken about the daggers in her glance earlier.

"I'll drink to that," Diego said, picking up his knife and clinking it against his glass. "Now we hear from *el capitán?*"

People joined him, clinking knives against glasses. Captain Pappas, put on the spot, stood and raised his glass.

"Welcome, everyone! The crew of *Alexandra's Dream* is delighted to have you aboard." He nodded to the diners and took a sip of his wine before again taking his seat.

The captain's gorgeous companion started the applause, her gold bracelets jangling. Soon the clinking against glasses was picked up by the rest of the room.

"Speech, speech, speech! We'd like to hear more from the captain."

Patti Kennedy took over and was joined by the maître d'. On behalf of the captain they delivered an amusing and upbeat welcome aboard. When Patti sat down there was a burst of applause. Serena caught the wink Thanasi sent her and Patti's blushing reaction.

The introductions began. Thanasi explained that he'd started off as bar manager and worked his way up to his current position. Then he nodded at Serena.

"Your turn, Ms. d'Andrea," he said.

Serena mentioned she was from Buenos Aires and published young adult and children's books.

And even though Marc LeClair kept his eyes on his wineglass, she knew he was looking at her.

The older couple were farmers from the Midwest, and the officer who'd arrived with Thanasi was the new staff captain. Diego turned out to be a competitive dancer who'd recently turned pro. And Helena, the beauty at the head of the table, was the captain's fiancée.

When it was Patti Kennedy's turn, she told the group that she had started on ships in a purser's capacity, and after mastering several languages, she'd moved up the ranks to Cruise Director.

Now only a few people were left to be introduced, Marc LeClair being one of them.

"My turn," Sal Morena said, baring his capped teeth and looking directly at Serena. "I am Salvatore Morena and I am originally from Genoa. There we are shipbuilders." He raised his eyebrows suggestively. "I am an escort, hired to dance with the ladies."

Carajo! There would be no way she could avoid him now. Sal had been hired to partner the female dancers. She'd better get to work quickly and find herself a partner or he'd be clinging to her like a cheap leotard.

Now it was Marc LeClair's turn, and Serena focused her full attention on him. He was still studiously avoiding making eye contact.

"I'm Gilles Anderson," he said in his sexy baritone. "I'm from Alberta, Canada, originally, and I'm on this cruise for a little R&R, and to learn to dance the tango like a pro."

Unable to stop herself, Serena blurted, "Gilles, do you have a twin brother?" Every eye at the table focused on her.

"Not that I know of. I'm the only boy in my family." He gave her another slow, lazy smile. That smile was familiar. How could she forget that cleft in his chin? What kind of sick game was he playing?

While everyone was thinking about dessert, an officer with a serious expression approached the table. He whispered something in Thanasi's ear. The hotel director was out of his seat in an instant, loping toward Captain Pappas.

"Thank you for what you did earlier," Serena said to Marc. "May I buy you a drink later?"

"That's not necessary, but I'll be in the Emperor's Club after the show. How about joining me?"

"Yes, I just might do that."

She couldn't wait. Serena planned on asking some very direct questions and seeing how he reacted to them.

CHAPTER SIX

SWEAT TRICKLED from Sal Morena's armpits and down his sides. He should have known better than to hand off a job requiring some finesse to a petty thief. Now he had to make sure that cabin steward didn't blab what little he knew.

Earlier, Sal had wandered into the crew area and found the employee going through the unclaimed passenger bags. He'd watched him stuff several items in his pockets before skulking away. Then, and only then, had Sal made his presence known.

The steward had almost had a cow when Sal approached him. Before he could open his mouth, the employee had begun babbling excuses about one of the passengers missing his bags. He'd supposedly been sent to look for them.

"What's in your pockets?" Sal asked him.

"Oh, these, I'm just taking some stuff back to see if the guests can identify it."

Sal could smell the lies a mile away, and the fear. The man's teeth were practically chattering. A fine layer of perspiration dotted his skin. Sal then moved in for the kill, threatening to expose the employee for the thief that he was, unless he found and brought him the pendant.

Fearing the loss of his job, the man had readily agreed to the plan. But Sal couldn't believe the idiot would attack the d'Andrea woman in public. What a moron! He was on a cruise ship with no place to go.

Sal had been counting the minutes until this dinner ended. Tracy, whom he suspected of sleeping with the new first officer, had managed to wangle him an invitation to the captain's table. Unfortunately, he'd been seated at the far end, away from the d'Andrea babe, and had been forced to chat up the old broad.

In the middle of dessert, Sal had seen the officer approach and whisper in the ear of the hotel director. The arrogant idiot had bolted from his seat as if someone had put a cattle prod to him. He'd gone up to the commander and whispered. Both men had then hot-footed it out of there. Something was definitely going down.

Alarm bells went off in Sal's head. The cabin steward didn't know his name, but he knew what Sal looked like. If the guy began to yap it would only be a matter of time before he was caught, and he couldn't afford to have that happen. Sal had dangled a bunch of crisp U.S. bills in front of the steward's nose and explained what he needed. He'd told the man to show up on the Observation Deck at midnight with the pendant, or there would be consequences.

Sal had thought the fool would use his master

key to enter the heiress's suite and search for the necklace.

Something would have to be done between now and tomorrow to shut up the little weasel. Coming to a decision, Sal kissed the wrinkled hand of the old cow he'd been flattering and stood.

"I hope you will forgive me, but tomorrow I am needed at a dance workshop at eight o'clock sharp."

"You haven't finished dessert," the old biddy reminded him, actually looking disappointed.

"A case of my eyes being larger than my stomach." He brought the dowager's hand to his mouth again. "The next time we meet we shall dance."

The thought of dancing with him pacified the old girl. She gave him a big smile. Implants for teeth, Sal thought as he left the table.

He bypassed the elevators—guaranteed to take too long at this hour—and bounded down the stairs two at a time. Tracy would be between performances and, with luck, back in her cabin. Sal's position as an escort gave him access to crew and passenger areas.

As he made his way down to a lower deck, he marveled at how quickly the scenery deteriorated the lower you got. Fantasy might be played out above, but reality was here in the form of dull, serviceable carpeting and drab gray walls.

He'd poked his head in a few of the open crew cabins earlier. There was nothing pretty about them. They reminded him of prison cells, minimally furnished with the requisite beds, in some cases bunks, and sterile at best. He'd gotten lucky being assigned the cabin he had.

"Who are you looking for?" A man dressed in shorts and a polo shirt who had been tending bar earlier, stopped to look at Sal curiously.

"Tracy Irvine. I have a message for her."

"Dark-haired woman, about this high. Nice figure." The bartender made a figure eight motion with his hands.

"That's the one."

"Three doors down and to your right."

Sal thanked him and moved on. In a matter of seconds he was at his ex-wife's door. He knocked lightly. No point in drawing attention to himself. When there was no response Sal tried again, this time harder. He heard someone rustling around inside and decided to hell with the subtle approach.

"It's Sal. Open up."

No answer.

"*Bella,* I need to talk to you. It's about last night." He spoke louder this time. "Don't leave me standing in the hallway screaming our business."

It had gotten very quiet. She must have an eye to the peephole. Using the tip of his shoe, he kicked at the door.

"Come on, *bella,* let me in. I'm sorry the condom broke. What did the doctor say about prescribing a morning after pill?"

That did it. The cabin door flew open. Tracy wore full makeup and a skimpy costume exposing a lot of skin.

"Do you have to be so gross, Sal?"

"*Ciao, bella.* You ain't seen nothing yet." He pushed his way into the room. "If you opened the door when I first knocked it wouldn't have to be like this."

Remnants of mascara rimmed Tracy's eyes. Her nose was red and swollen. She'd been crying, probably missing Franco, who was perfectly safe in Genoa with his nonna. Tracy didn't need to know that.

"Why are you here?" she asked, her arms crossed protectively over her chest, deepening her cleavage.

Sal flopped onto the narrow twin bed. He lay back and folded his hands under his head.

"I need you to take care of something for me."

She didn't answer, just continued to look at him.

"The moron I hired managed to get caught. I need to know where he is. I can't risk him saying too much."

Tracy looked simultaneously horrified and petrified.

"You were behind that attack? You had that woman choked?"

Sal sat up and planted his feet on the industrial carpeting. "Just get me the information I need. Find out where that stupid steward is being kept and report back to me on the double."

"But Sal…"

"But Sal nothing. I'll be waiting behind the smoke stack after the last show. You better have information for me, or you can forget about seeing Franco again."

"I'm his mother," Tracy wailed, tears streaking

what was left of her makeup. "I need to see my child."

Sal slid off the bed and came toward her. He could smell the clammy scent of fear on her skin, that and an exotic perfume. His ex-wife was still an attractive, shapely babe but she'd been difficult to manage.

Sal reached over and fondled a breast. He held the soft flesh in one hand, inhaling her while licking his lips.

"Sal, please don't."

He felt her recoil, shudder. No one treated Salvatore Morena as if he were day-old fish. He tweaked Tracy's nipple hard and smiled as she winced.

"Ouch!"

When she began crying in earnest, he pressed his advantage.

"I need that information, and I need it yesterday, *capisce?*"

"I understand."

She was finally getting it.

Then again, maybe not. He'd known he couldn't depend on her. She'd screwed up time and time again.

"YOU'RE ON YOUR OWN tonight," Pia said to Serena while they were walking along the promenade on Bacchus after the show.

"Are you going to bed already?" Retiring early was so unlike Pia.

An after-show crowd, out to party, was already sashaying back and forth. The promenade was a central gathering area, the place to see and be seen. Inside the casino, the chi-chink of slot machines and the shouts of an inebriated crowd floated their way. The gaming tables were packed to overflowing.

"I have a date," Pia announced, sounding quite pleased with herself.

"With whom?"

"Andreas. I'm meeting him on the Observation Deck when he gets off duty." Pia glanced at her watch. "Which is about now. Will you be all right on your own?"

"Of course. I'll be at the Emperor's Club." When Pia hiked an eyebrow, Serena explained, "It's really the wine and cigar bar. I'm supposed to meet Marc there."

"Have a good time, *querida,* and don't stay out too late. We have an early coaching session tomorrow with one of the top instructors."

"I haven't forgotten."

As Pia hustled toward the elevators, Serena headed off in the opposite direction. She took her time, stopping to peek in at the many boutiques that sold everything from delicate crystal to formal clothing. She was excited by the prospect of meeting up with Marc again.

Despite what he said, she was certain that he was the man she'd spent two weeks dancing with and making love to. Those midnight-blue eyes and that shock of dark hair had left an impression, and so had the cleft in his chin.

"We will make this work somehow," he'd said

toward the end of the last week. "Colombia isn't that far away."

"No, it's not, but it might as well be the end of the world. Who will I dance with after this week ends?"

She'd been close to tears, and they both knew it had little to do with losing her dance partner and more about missing the man she'd fallen in love with.

"A beautiful woman like you will always have plenty of dance partners," Marc had said, cupping her chin and forcing her to look at him. "And I will be jealous of each and every one of them. We're not over, Serena, not by a long shot."

Liar! He'd crept out like a thief in the middle of the night, leaving her lying in bed, and never looked back.

Now she didn't want to appear too anxious, or give Marc the impression she couldn't wait to see him. This would be as good a time as any to explore more of the public areas. Tomorrow's session was scheduled in the Polaris Lounge, but she still hadn't seen The Rose Petal tearoom, which also served as an after dinner meeting place.

Serena quickly made her way there. The room was decorated like an English garden, and while some might consider it fussy, she thought it had great style with its chintz furnishings and pretty lace-covered tables. A large gold harp was positioned in one corner, and ivy and cabbage roses blossomed from the gigantic Chinese vases and urns positioned throughout.

On a far wall, a portrait of a blonde woman, her

hair piled high and secured by a comb, caught her attention. The woman was regal looking, with an inner strength emanating from her. The mythical moon goddess perhaps?

Serena came closer to stare up at the beautiful woman. An aura of tranquility wrapped around her like a cloak, but the twinkle in her eye indicated that there were more layers to her than the artist could possibly capture.

She wore a striking gown in a beautiful shade of aquamarine, and a silver bracelet was clasped around one slender wrist. A tear-shaped diamond pendant was nestled between her creamy breasts.

Serena clutched her purse to her, reassuring herself her own silver pendant was still in it. The one this woman wore had a similar shape.

Eager to find out who the enchanting woman was, Serena scanned the accompanying plaque, reading the words out loud.

"In Memory of Alexandra Rhys-Williams Stamos— My Own Moon Goddess."

"*Muy hermosa,* isn't she?"

Turning, Serena spotted Diego Montalban. "Yes, she is beautiful."

Diego had come into the room accompanied by others who were probably from the dance group. They carried drinks with them. He stood next to Serena, gazing up at the portrait while his friends circled the room, oohing and ahhing.

"You think she was happy with him?" Diego asked.

"Who is she?"

"She was the owner's wife, an Englishwoman. Elias Stamos, the shipping magnate, met her when she was on holiday in Greece. They had a whirlwind courtship and she bore him two daughters."

"In that case, I'd think she was very happy. Look at the way her eyes sparkle and her mouth curves up when she smiles. Look at her complexion, all peaches and cream."

"The work of an excellent makeup artist or a master portrait maker, perhaps," Diego said drolly.

Serena couldn't help laughing. She was enjoying the exchange and enjoying Diego. "Don't ruin it for me," she answered. "Allow me to fantasize."

As frequently happened, a vivid image of her twin, Selena, flashed through her mind. At times she missed her so much, her heart actually ached. Selena would have enjoyed the ship and all the activities. She would especially have loved Diego, as irreverent as he was.

Tomorrow, Serena vowed, she would find someplace quiet and start drafting that book. She had been putting it off for far too long, and she owed it to Selena's memory to write that story.

"Come back to me." Diego's voice penetrated Serena's thoughts.

"She died so young. Do you know what happened?" Serena asked.

"No. But it was not something she planned, I am sure. Now let's talk about something more pleasant, like convincing you to dance with me."

"I'd love to dance with you. I'm taking a class tomorrow at the crack of dawn, and I'll be at the group party later."

The twang of the harp caught their attention. One of Diego's friends had struck a silly pose while fooling around.

"A little too much grappa perhaps," Diego muttered. "I better go and rescue that instrument." He loped away, calling over his shoulder, "We'll catch up at the group dance for sure. Tomorrow morning I'm going scuba diving. Enjoy your night."

After circling the room again, Serena made her way out. She poked a head in the library, admiring the warm wood and comfortable seating, and the shelves filled with book after book.

Serena stepped inside and walked over to one of the shelves. Her hands trailed the spines of several well known classics. Selena would have been in seventh heaven, she thought. The library would be the perfect place to get started on this book. But not tonight—tonight she was on a totally different mission.

A crowd of people were sampling truffles at Temptations, the Chocolate Café, when Serena went by. A few sipped on champagne. What she wouldn't do for a strawberry dipped in chocolate. Too bad she couldn't afford the calories.

She'd wasted enough time and could now make her fashionably late entrance. The pungent smell of rich tobacco indicated she was nearing the club. The aroma was something she always associated with her father, who made a point of having a cigar every night. He said it relaxed him.

The club was filled with a diverse group of people, ranging from officers to women on the prowl. Serena scanned the crowd, hoping to find Marc already seated, but couldn't spot him. There wasn't a vacant table to be found so she approached the bar. She'd have a glass of red wine, wait a few minutes to see if he would show up, and then move on.

She was about to place her order when she felt a tap on her shoulder. Serena swung around and came face-to-face with the man she was looking for.

"There you are," Marc LeClair said, a mischievous twinkle in his eyes indicating he was pleased to see her. The cleft in his chin was even deeper than she remembered. He held a cup of dark liquid in his hand. "The hotel and cruise directors were here only a minute ago, and then they got paged and went rushing off somewhere. I thought you'd stood me up so I went to the Espresso Bar to drown my sorrows. Shall we try to find seats?"

"Stood up" implied they were on a date. He couldn't possibly be thinking of picking up where they had left off.

"There's no place to sit," she said, refusing to acknowledge her quickening pulse and the heightened awareness of the man standing beside her. Marc wore an open-necked shirt with the sleeves rolled up to reveal tanned, corded forearms. His dress slacks were immaculately pressed with a sharp crease to them, and his tasseled, leather loafers were shiny. He smelled like an exotic Asian spice. And just like she remembered.

"If I can get hold of a waiter I'll order us drinks and we can take them to the library," Marc suggested.

"I promised to buy you a drink," Serena reminded him.

"You can get the next one."

Ten minutes later they were seated on one of the library's leather couches, brandy snifters in hand.

"With the exception of that earlier unpleasant incident, are you enjoying yourself?" Marc asked when they'd settled in.

"Oh, yes. The show was wonderful, like being in Las Vegas, I'm told. The dancers were beautiful women and very talented."

"None as stunning as you. Have you been to Las Vegas?"

Serena smiled back at him. She was beginning to get a warm, tingly feeling all over, but she attributed it to the drink and not Marc's presence.

"You're too kind," she said. "No I've never been to Las Vegas. Have you?"

"Yes, on business."

"Tell me about it."

Marc described the ornate five-star hotels, and the highly rated restaurants. He told her about the glitzy shows, the top-rated performers, and of course the gambling.

"It's a fun place to visit but I'm not sure I'd want to live there," he added. "And it's definitely not a place to raise kids."

"Do you have children?" Serena eyed him over the rim of her brandy snifter.

"Yes, one daughter." He didn't elaborate further.

The cognac was beginning to loosen her tongue.

"And where is this daughter of yours?"

"She lives with her mother."

Serena was going by pure intuition. But the more they spoke, the more she was convinced this was Marc. She'd spent enough time with him to note a couple of personal habits, like the way he outlined the cleft of his chin with one finger when he was thinking. Marc was doing exactly that right now.

She reached over and placed a hand on his arm. "Are you sure you have never visited my country?"

His dreamy blue eyes drifted over her. "I've forgotten which country that is?"

"Argentina. Buenos Aires."

"And you ask because…?"

"You remind me of a man I was involved with."

"And if I were this man, why would I pretend not to know you?"

"Only you can answer that."

A couple came wandering into the library. They were holding hands and talking quietly

"Isn't the ship beautiful?" the woman said, crossing over to admire one of the paintings on the wall.

"It certainly is," her companion agreed.

They circled the room several times before taking a seat on an adjacent couch.

"We thought we'd have a quick aperitif before

going to the piano bar," the man said. "The pianist is awesome."

Marc took Serena's almost empty glass from her and set it down on the table. He stood and held out his hand.

"And we're on our way to the Polaris Lounge to listen to big band music. Maybe we'll even dance."

Serena accepted the hand he offered and stood. She hadn't been expecting an evening of dancing. But now she would know for sure whether Gilles Anderson and Marc LeClair were one and the same.

Two different people would not have identical moves.

CHAPTER SEVEN

"HOW IS THAT POSSIBLE? How could a man simply disappear into thin air?" Nick Pappas asked, pacing the circumference of his spacious quarters.

"We will find him, Captain," Sean Brady quickly assured him. "There's no way a man can just disappear off a ship."

"I guess you haven't been reading the newspapers lately," Nick muttered, adjusting the drawstring of his pajama bottoms. "This seems to be happening more and more—people going missing and never turning up."

Thanasi had asked Sean the same question. How could this be happening? They'd both been reluctant to awaken Nick at this god-awful hour, but they had no choice. Elias Stamos had to be called at his vacation home in Barbados before the incident made the newspapers.

The port of Key West was already visible. The minute they docked, and even before the ship officially cleared, the police and authorities would be swarming the vessel. How to explain the disappearance of a man who'd been locked up with two security guards posted out front?

Sean had reported that when one of the security officers, accompanied by a busboy, had gone to the brig to bring Milutin Krupinsky his breakfast, the guards were nowhere to be found. They'd figured the guards were either on a break or using the facilities. When they'd unlocked the door, the brig was empty, and that's when panic set in.

There'd been no signs of forced entry or evidence of foul play. They'd waited around for a while but the security guards never returned, and that's when they'd sounded the alarm.

"Thanasi," Nick ordered, "get Elias Stamos on the phone."

"At this hour, Captain?"

Thanasi and Nick were good friends and had some shared history, but out of respect the hotel director always referred to the commander by his title, especially when others were around.

"It has to be done. Use my phone." Nick gestured to a telephone on a small desk. "Elias's number is on the bulletin board right above my desk. If necessary, get the ship-to-shore operator to put through the call. The moment Elias gets on the line I'll take over. I'm off to throw water on my face and get dressed."

Nick Pappas had been sleeping the sleep of the dead when they'd knocked on his door and woken him up. Thanasi suspected his lovely fiancée, Helena, Elias's daughter, was with him, rather than in the penthouse suite family members often used. Helena had flown in from London and boarded the ship in Fort Lauderdale. She'd been showing up more frequently these past few voyages.

Thanasi and Sean now entered the captain's comfortable quarters. It held the requisite desk and computer. A sofa was positioned against one wall facing a silent television. Racks held a collection of sports and automobile magazines, and framed black and white photographs of various ports of call hung on the far wall.

Elias Stamos's number was exactly where Nick said it would be, on the bulletin board and directly at eye level. Thanasi picked up the receiver and punched in the numbers that would get him through to the owner's vacation home. Elias spent a few months of the winter in Barbados, but the rest of the year ran the business in his beloved Greece.

The phone rang for what seemed an eternity. Finally a female picked up, her voice heavy with sleep. Elias Stamos's new woman most likely. Sadie Bennett was the mother of Ariana, the ship's librarian.

"This is Thanasi Kaldis, Hotel Director on *Alexandra's Dream,* calling for Mr. Stamos. I'm sorry for the late call but it is important."

"Do you know what time it is?" the woman asked. "Mr. Stamos is sleeping."

"I'm calling on behalf of Captain Nick Pappas. He needs to speak to Mr. Stamos right away."

"What's going on, Sadie?" a man's muffled voice asked in the background.

Several seconds of silence followed. Thanasi

guessed a hand had been placed over the mouthpiece while Sadie explained what was going on.

"Nick, tell me there is not another situation," the owner's querulous voice demanded.

"Not Nick, sir. Thanasi Kaldis, Hotel Director."

"Put Nick on."

"He'll be with you shortly." Now it was Thanasi's turn to cover the mouthpiece as he went to the bathroom door. "Captain Pappas, Mr. Stamos is asking to speak with you."

"I'll be right out."

Nick emerged shortly thereafter, this time fully clothed. He took the receiver from Thanasi and barked into it, "Elias, how are you? Sorry to be calling at such a ridiculous hour. Yes, it's important—"

Elias must have cut him off, because Nick listened for a while, his jaw clenching and unclenching.

"It's worse than that," he said when he could get a word in. "When I called you earlier I mentioned a newly hired crew member had publicly assaulted a woman. We put him in the brig figuring he would be secure until we could turn him over to the police. Now he's disappeared."

Another long drawn out silence followed as Elias spoke.

"Yes, the police and other authorities will be boarding soon. And no, I don't have any idea how we can possibly keep this out of the media."

More silence followed.

"Yes, I understand you perfectly, sir. Let me see what I can do."

He hung up the phone. Thanasi noted the effort it was taking for Nick to pull himself together. He must have gotten quite the dressing down from Elias Stamos. The ship's owner would soon be Nick's father-in-law, and Elias had handpicked Nick to Captain *Alexandra's Dream,* but business was business, and Elias could be a tough son of a gun. He was probably holding Nick fully responsible for the crew member's disappearance.

Once the authorities boarded, things would get uglier.

"What can we do, Captain?" Sean Brady asked, breaking the awkward silence.

"Get every security person you have on the case. I want them to search every inch of this ship and some. You have half an hour before we drop anchor, maybe a little less."

"I'll do that, sir."

Sean's beeper went off. He was heading for the door when a loud banging came from the other side. All three men jumped, reacting to the sound.

"Shall I get it, Captain?" Sean asked.

"Sure. Hopefully it's good news and that petty crook has been found."

Sean yanked open the door and faced the Staff Captain and Tom Diamantopoulos, the Chief Engineer.

"We've got another situation," Tom said, looking harried. Both men were beet-red and their expressions indicated that there were big problems.

Thanasi and Nick exchanged looks. They'd

worked long enough together to know what the other was thinking.

"What's going on?" Nick addressed the question to the Staff Captain.

"Captain, one of the cleaners found the missing security guards on the observation deck. They were locked into a utility closet, both were bound and drugged."

"What!" Thanasi couldn't help the outburst.

"Where are my men now?" Sean asked, stepping into the role of interrogator.

"They've been taken to the infirmary."

"Wait, there's more," Tom, the chief engineer said, a grim expression on his sharp features.

"More?" Nick's thumb worried the flesh between his eyes.

"Security did a quick walk around the Observation Deck. They found a pair of men's shoes close to the railing, lined up neatly as if someone had stepped out of them."

"And you're thinking?" Thanasi said, although he already knew what they were thinking.

"We may have a man overboard," Tom explained. "We've already done a cabin search but no one's come up missing except that steward. Our conclusion is he jumped or was pushed overboard."

"And why would he take off his shoes?" Sean asked, raising a skeptical eyebrow. His beeper made another buzzing sound. "With your permission, Captain, I'd like to head down to the infirmary and see what's going on."

Nick inclined his head. "Notify me the minute you find out anything."

Sean slipped through the open door and Nick picked up the phone again.

"I'm going to have to call Elias again with this latest update. Get a hold of the emergency numbers and contact the Vice President of Port Operations. He'll need to alert the PR Department and Guest Relations at headquarters. Make sure to brief Patti, the chief purser, and all key personnel. The moment this news breaks, reporters are going to descend on this ship like maggots. We've got maybe ten minutes left before we dock."

"Will do, Captain."

By the time Thanasi reached Patti Kennedy she was already briefing the Guest Relations staff and the accountants on duty. She had organized a small group of entertainers to act as backup to aid with crowd control.

The news would soon spread and passengers would panic. Some would be looking to get off in Key West, and quite a few would storm the front desk, demanding a spokesperson from headquarters and additional security be put in place.

"Would you like to take over and give us an update?" she asked, relinquishing her spot center stage.

Thanasi doubted that she'd had more than three or four hours sleep, if that, but Patti still looked crisp and fresh. Her hair was pulled off her face in a high ponytail and she wasn't wearing makeup. She'd thrown on a pair of slacks and a polo shirt with the ship's logo on the pocket, foregoing her usual crisp, buttoned-down look.

He quickly updated the crew, telling them what he knew. He reminded them that they were to remain calm and professional, regardless of what was said to them. They were not to speculate about the circumstances with passengers.

"Customs and immigrations will be boarding the ship soon," Thanasi reminded them. "Your job is to make sure the passenger list, passports and visas are ready for inspection. You are to keep passengers calm. We'll keep you informed when we learn something more." He nodded to Patti, indicating he was done. When she stepped back into place he lowered his voice, adding, "I'm heading to the infirmary to see what's going on with those men. Are you okay to handle things on your own?"

"Absolutely. Beep me if you need me."

Thanasi wanted to speak to the two guards before the police and authorities boarded. Once that happened, the guards would be intimidated and start demanding lawyers. Sean was probably on the same wavelength, which was why he'd gone down to the infirmary.

At the most it would be another few minutes before the ship anchored, and the passengers began clamoring to disembark. Key West with its quaint homes and colorful watering holes was a popular destination. Everyone wanted to ride the trolleys, shop the overpriced stores and frequent Sloppy Joe's, the restaurant/bar made famous by Ernest Hemingway.

The doors of the infirmary were closed as Thanasi approached. He got out his walkie talkie and spoke into it.

"Sean come in, please. Come in, Sean."

A crackling static went on for seconds until finally Sean came on the other end, "Where are you Thanasi?"

"In the hallway, in front of the infirmary. Open up the door."

"Hang on."

The door of the infirmary pushed open, and an attendant stood aside. Sean and another guard paced the small waiting area.

"Where's the doctor?" Thanasi asked.

Sean jutted a thumb in the direction of an inner room.

"Were you able to talk to the two men?"

"Not exactly."

"What does not exactly mean?"

"They're still pretty doped up and not making much sense. Doc thinks someone put a hypodermic needle to them. They were out like a light."

"Great. Make sure you've got your security reports in order for the police. You know the drill. We're about to port into Key West any minute. Captain Pappas is going to need my help so I've got to get back up to his cabin. Beep me when you need me."

Sean assured him that he would

With that Thanasi bounded off. He knew the drill, too. All hell was about to break loose.

MARC STOOD ON THE sundeck, an arm looped around Serena's shoulders. A light mist hovered over the water, and the outline of what looked to be a hotel could be seen in the distance amidst a number of low buildings. After reading the literature in his cabin he couldn't wait to tour Key West.

He was looking forward to exploring every inch of the port with the woman beside him, although he wondered if that was smart. Spending any time with Serena might be endangering her life.

There was a contract out on Marc's life, and he would not put it past the drug lord who had threatened him to go after anyone who got close to him.

Call him selfish, but after dancing away the night with Serena, he'd been reluctant to have their time together end. He was enjoying getting reacquainted.

"Tired?" he asked her, tucking a strand of escaping hair behind her ear.

"Happy tired."

Serena stood barefoot, holding the straps of her high-heeled sandals in one hand. All that glorious jet-black hair was nestled on his shoulders.

"Don't you have a dance class right after breakfast?" Marc asked.

"Yes, I signed up for private instructions. In Argentina our day often starts at midnight. We are used to being up all night."

Although it had been six months, his memories of being up all night were still vivid. He and Serena had watched many a sunrise together. From the moment they'd met at that night club and she'd encouraged him to sign on for what remained of the two-week dance clinic, they'd practically spent every waking moment together.

He'd been so glad he'd decided to take that trip to Buenos Aires to meet with his colleagues from the Canadian embassy. But he hadn't been exactly truthful with Serena about his profession. He'd told her he was a businessman and she'd accepted that without question.

Marc stifled a yawn. The effects of too many drinks and too little rest were beginning to take their toll. A few hours sleep might give him a lift.

"After your dance class what will you do?" he asked.

"Go ashore and browse the stores. Maybe find the sandal factory. What will you do?"

"Get a couple of hours of shut eye, and then take a nice long walk around town. I'm considering snorkeling or taking a taxi and going to another key. Right now I want to do this."

Dipping his head, Marc kissed her. For one fraction of a moment the world came to a standstill. Serena d'Andrea tasted just as he remembered. Delicious.

When he finally came up for breath, Serena's lyrical tones filled his ear, "How about I join you?"

"I'd love it."

It was an offer only a fool would refuse.

CHAPTER EIGHT

WHEN SERENA ENTERED the Polaris Lounge, Pia was already on the wooden floor dancing with the instructor.

"You're late," her friend said, her raised eyebrows and slightly pursed lips indicating she would be quizzing the heck out of Serena later.

"By ten minutes," Serena answered, tapping the face of her watch. "Sorry."

Knowing that she had this dance lesson scheduled, she'd said goodbye to Marc and rushed to her suite for a quick shower and change of clothing. When there wasn't any sign of Pia, Serena assumed that she was already at breakfast.

"Good morning," called the instructor, a man of medium height and build. "We started a few minutes ago. Go ahead and warm up."

Serena joined them on the dance floor doing a series of stretches to loosen up. She began dancing in place while watching the instructor's mastery of an intricate tango step.

"Why warm up by yourself, when you can warm up with me?" a voice called from behind her.

She turned to see Sal Morena dressed all in black, striking a dramatic pose. His arms were wide open and all his weight appeared to be on his left foot.

Was he following her, or did his duties as gentleman host encompass partnering students taking private dance lessons? Regardless, she didn't want to dance with him. But to walk away, or simply ignore him would be rude.

The instructor, perhaps sensing her dilemma, approached.

"You dance with Ms. Fischer," he said to Sal, "and I will work with Ms. d'Andrea."

Turning Pia over to Sal, the instructor began a forward walk. Turning both palms up and wiggling his fingers, he encouraged Serena to imitate him.

Serena had always loved the seductive music of the tango. She shook her flowing mane and did her best to imitate the instructor.

For the next forty-five minutes, the instructor alternated his teaching between Serena and Pia. Sal quickly stepped in when she needed a partner but she was having a difficult time following him, and she no longer felt the music. There was something about the man that put her off, although on the surface he seemed pleasant enough.

"Well, that's it for this morning," the instructor announced. "You both did very well. Now you may go ashore and sightsee, maybe do a little shopping. Key West is a charming little town—you'll enjoy it."

"You dance beautifully," Sal added, bowing

slightly. "Should you lovely ladies need an escort to show you around Key West, I am your man."

Over Serena's dead body. Yet both women smiled graciously and made as graceful an exit as they could.

On the way to their suite, they encountered passengers conversing in loud tones.

"So did you hear about the man who jumped overboard?"

"Yes, I heard he was pushed."

"They say only his shoes were found."

"Could be the same guy who disappeared from the brig."

"And what about those security guards who were found tied up and drugged."

"What about them?"

"I came on a cruise to rest and relax—who expected this much drama?"

"The police are on board now. The captain needs to make an announcement and tell us what's going on. I'm scared to death. What if I'm next?"

Serena and Pia exchanged looks but waited until they were back in their suite to talk.

"Do you think what those people were saying is true?" Pia asked, tossing off her shoes and flopping down on the bed.

"What part? The man going overboard, or the drugged security guards?"

"All of it. The police, the man escaping from the brig, the drugged guards. *Dios mío,* I feel like I am in a bad movie."

Serena pulled the tight-fitting jersey dress over her head, stripped off her underwear and flung them on a chair. She was not the neatest of people and right now the shortage of sleep was starting to catch up with her.

Pia, in a spurt of energy, bounded off the bed and began going through the drawers.

"I can't find my new swimsuit."

"Second drawer from the bottom," Serena answered, climbing under the covers and pulling them up over her head. "Are you going to the pool or the beach?"

"All I know is that I'm getting off this ship as soon as I can. I'm going to the beach with the people I met last night."

"What about Andreas?" Serena asked, already half-asleep.

"He's on duty. By the way, if you leave I'd take that pendant with you. I've got this gut feeling that there's more to it than just a piece of molten silver."

"You might be right," Serena answered, drifting off.

"How did it go?" Ariana Bennett, the ship's librarian, closed the bridal magazine she'd been leafing through.

"As good as these things ever do," Patti Kennedy said. "We're lucky to still be in the United States where there's some protocol for handling criminals."

"I suppose you're right. At least here people have rights and are able to get an attorney, and you can count on the FBI to get involved."

"True."

The library was currently closed since it was presumed the vast majority of passengers would want to get off in Key West. Ariana had been debating what to do with these precious few moments when Patti, looking totally exhausted, had tapped on the locked library door.

They'd become good friends and recognized each other as kindred spirits. A woman in Patti's position needed support. As the sole female officer, she didn't have it easy. It took a strong-minded individual to hold her own with arrogant, testosterone-driven men.

Patti kicked off her pumps and threw herself on one of the leather sofas.

"Did you find a wedding dress for the shipboard ceremony?"

"Not yet. I plan on keeping it fairly simple. I thought maybe I'd pick something up on the French side of St. Maarten. Something cool and made of Sea Island cotton, strapless but comfortable. My mom ordered the traditional formal gown with the trailing veil from New York. I'll wear that for the Philly wedding."

"It's nice she's so involved. It can't be easy trying to plan a wedding from a ship. How is Sadie, anyway?" Patti asked. Mother and daughter had grown closer after Ariana had mysteriously disappeared. Sadie had come looking for her and spent time aboard *Alexandra's Dream* getting to know the crew, and ended up falling for the big cheese himself, Elias Stamos.

Ariana removed her glasses and tossed them on the table in front of her. Her blue eyes sparkled impishly as she responded.

"My mother is in love. As we speak, she's at Elias's vacation home in Barbados. The two seem to be a match made in heaven. He dotes on her."

"I'm happy for them."

Patti's beeper vibrated. She glanced at the number, and shot up.

"Gotta go. The Chief Mucka-Mucka is calling."

"Chief Mucka-Mucka as in Captain Pappas, or our gorgeous workaholic of a hotel director? In case you haven't noticed, he's hot for you."

"He is not."

"Then you're the only one who doesn't know it. Just look at how red you've gotten."

Patti knew her flushed face was a sure giveaway. How crazy was this, blushing like an adolescent whenever Thanasi's name came up?

"I have to go," she said, racing out the door. "Let's have a drink at the crew bar later."

"I'm holding you to it," Ariana called after her. "We're both overdue for a night off."

"I hear you."

Her beeper vibrated again and Patti raced off.

ON ATHENA, MARC PACED the Liberty Plaza where the reception and concierge desks were located. It was the place where passengers came to book shore excursions and future cruises. He'd promised to meet Serena here in the hotel lobby. Since it was a little after midday, he hoped that she hadn't already eaten.

While he'd waited, he had used the computers in the Internet Café to research what there was to do in Key West. He'd gotten a map from the employees selling shore excursions and was excited about exploring Old Town and grabbing a quick bite at Sloppy Joe's.

As he stood impatiently waiting, the hotel director, a stony expression on his face, stormed by. He had a group of serious-looking men flanking him.

"Hey, you," a female voice called. Before Marc could respond, he was enveloped in a cloud of perfume and squished against Heddy, the woman he'd been dancing with.

Marc tried to disentangle himself. Heddy smelled of sand, sun, and rum. She wore a skimpy bikini top in a Stars and Stripes pattern, and everything she owned popped over the stars that barely covered her nipples. Circling her hips was a floral sarong. Her pierced belly button sported a gold lock with a tiny key. High-heeled wedges brought her almost eye-level to him, and she carried one of those silly rattan bags that had flowers blooming on the front.

"Oops!" she said when one star shifted, exposing a puckered nipple. She took her time tucking her breast back into place.

Marc thought it best to pretend the incident never happened. Where was Serena?

"I'm thinking of getting myself a tattoo, right here," Heddy said, pointing to the space between her cleavage. "You could come ashore with me and help me pick out something sexy."

"Sounds tempting but unfortunately I have other plans."

On cue, his other plans came sailing up, looking as fresh as an ocean breeze, and smelling like it, too. Serena wore a pair of thigh-hugging shorts that stopped right above the knee and a halter top that was a tasteful contrast to the star spangled banner's scrap of cloth. Her hair was pulled back in a ponytail. She clutched a straw hat in one hand and a sensible-looking straw purse in the other.

"Sorry I'm late," she said, offering up her cheek for his kiss.

Marc dutifully kissed the smooth flesh, wishing that he was bold enough to claim her mouth instead, but the middle of the ship's lobby was not the place for this.

Heddy looked noticeably put out by Serena's arrival, but Serena took it all in stride. She stuck out a hand and grinned.

"*Hola*—hi. I'm Serena d'Andrea."

"Heather Maxwell. Aren't you the woman who got attacked on the dance floor?" Heddy asked grumpily.

"That's right," Serena replied.

"We should go," Marc said, taking her by the elbow.

"Maybe we'll run into each other in town and we can have a drink," Heddy called after them, looking directly at Marc.

Out of earshot, Serena said, "That woman is what you call bigger than life."

"Which part of her?"

Serena threw back her head and laughed as they walked down the ramp and onto the dock.

They were steps away from Mallory Square when Marc took Serena's hand. They followed a sign that said, "This Way to Old Town."

"Are you hungry?" he asked.

"Starving, but I want to see everything," she said, skipping alongside him.

Marc marveled at Serena's enthusiasm. It was the thing he liked about her most and what had attracted him to her in the first place. She was open and always up. In his work he was forced to be diplomatic and controlled, so he loved her spontaneity and zest for life.

"We've got a few hours before we need to get back on board for the group dance," he said. "Is there something special you'd like to do?"

"Spend it with you."

She'd earned herself ten points with that answer.

Marc took the map of Key West from his pocket.

"Let's go to Duval Street and grab something to eat at Sloppy Joe's, Hemingway's old hangout. Afterward we can take a walking tour, rent bikes or hop on the trolley."

"Food first, then."

"I love the way you think."

He followed the signs for Duval, reputed to be the longest street in the world. It had some of the better known bars and restaurants, places with names like Hogs Breath and Fat Tuesdays.

On the way, Serena stopped to poke her head into some of the tourist stores selling the usual trinkets.

She entered a little boutique that sold hats and Marc patiently watched as she tried on at least a dozen.

As they continued up the street, Serena's steps slowed. Her expression grew serious.

"I think someone is following us," she said, looking over her shoulder.

"Of course people are following us. The entire ship is. Every cruise passenger is on Duval. It's the big draw."

Although he'd made light of her concern, his caution buttons were on high. Had he been followed here? Could the man who'd threatened his life have found out he was on *Alexandra's Dream?* Was he endangering Serena's life by being with her? It was a frightening thought.

"It's not funny," Serena said, actually shuddering. "I had a creepy feeling inside the hat shop. And when I popped into that crowded card store I thought I saw someone ducking behind the displays."

They'd reached the corner of Greene and Duval. Judging by the noise coming from the interior of the building to their right, they were at the famous Sloppy Joe's.

"Yes, this is it," Marc announced, spotting the author's features painted on one of the hanging signs.

After sidestepping the crowd, they were told there were would be a fifteen minute wait before they were seated.

"Let's have a drink at The Lazy Gecko," Serena suggested, pointing to a place right next door.

"A woman after my own heart."

Marc playfully slapped Serena's back. He'd missed her. Their romance, although brief, had been memorable. Serena had brought a much needed spark to his staid and sometimes stuffy world. She'd loosened him up, urging him to go out and try new things. They'd gone up in a hot air balloon together and tried rock climbing, things he'd never done before. For two weeks she'd made him forget that his life was being threatened by a drug lord.

Holding her hand, Marc entered The Lazy Gecko. With several ships in port, the place was packed, and the bartenders were busy juggling customers. In a few minutes they were sipping on the Mojitas the female bartender had encouraged them to try.

"Ready for another?" he asked.

"Bring it on." Serena laughed, and her entire body laughed with her. "I learned that expression from one of my American authors."

How charming she was, and so real. No pretending with her. There had to be an explanation why she hadn't called him. They'd had a great time together, at least he'd thought so, and he'd left her a note with all his numbers on it.

Marc ordered another two Mojitas.

"To getting to know you better," he said.

"To having a new salsa and tango partner," Serena added, slyly eyeing him over the rim.

"I'm lousy at the rhythm dances, but I do smooth well."

"Yes, I know." She laughed, as if at some private joke.

Why did he get the feeling she wasn't buying his Gilles Anderson cover one bit?

He'd have to do something to ensure she did. His safety depended on it.

CHAPTER NINE

MARC TOSSED A HANDFUL of bills onto the bar. "Our fifteen minutes were up at least half an hour ago. Our table's probably gone."

"I hope not—I'm starving," Selena said.

At Sloppy Joe's Marc used his considerable charm to convince the hostess to seat them. It wasn't quite midafternoon, but many of the patrons were already drunk. He ordered a Sloppy Joe and Serena chose a hamburger, and when their food arrived, they ate in companionable silence as they people-watched.

It was Serena's suggestion they take the walking tour after lunch. While they walked, she told him all about her desire to write a young adult's book. She was going to use her time on the cruise to start it.

"Has writing always been a passion of yours?" Marc asked.

"Not really. I'm a publisher. My twin sister was the one with the dream. I want to write the book for her."

"What happened to your sister?"

"Selena died in an equestrian accident when she

was eighteen. She was my best friend, losing her was like losing a limb. It was like having my heart ripped out." The sharp pain of grief had dulled now to a constant ache. "My parents depend on me solely. They expect me to run the publishing house when they get old."

Marc gave her shoulder a sympathetic squeeze.

"I'm sorry. Your parents must have a great deal of confidence in you. Sure you're still up for a tour with a bunch of awed tourists? I have a map. We could explore on our own." He patted his pocket.

Serena suppressed her sadness and focused on the thought of time alone with Marc. She no longer felt as if they were being followed, either, so she could relax. Maybe Marc was right after all. With all the tourists in town, you could easily imagine some one trailing you.

"Let's hop the Conch Train and see where it takes us," she suggested.

"Okay. I want to see 322 Duval. It's the oldest house in Key West. It was turned into a Wreckers Museum."

"You're on."

For the next few hours they wandered the streets, taking the train or trolley whenever they felt like it. They admired the awesome architecture of the Strand Theater, and talked jokingly about stealing the tiles off the San Carlos Opera House. Then they strolled Upper Duval between South and Petronia, poking around Bahama Village and touring President Truman's former residence.

"My feet hurt like crazy," Serena admitted when they were on the street again.

"Do you want to go back to the ship?"

"Oh, no, not until I find the sandal factory, I want to buy a few pairs."

"Then I'll get a taxi."

Half a dozen pairs of sandals later, they were back on the ship. Serena touched Marc's arm lightly.

"What about a dip in the pool?"

"Good idea. How about we meet on Artemis in twenty minutes?"

"Twenty minutes it is."

Marc placed an arm around her waist and they walked through the lobby toward the bank of elevators. He gave her a quick kiss before getting off on the deck below hers.

Feeling invigorated and alive, Serena practically skipped down the hallway. The thought of spending time in an intimate setting with Marc had her hopeful he would admit who he was. Maybe he would tell her why he was traveling under an assumed name.

She was also looking forward to seeing him in his swim trunks. She'd fantasized about Marc's hard body and rippling muscles. She'd touched every inch of his skin with her hands and her mouth. She remembered clearly what his chest looked like with its mat of smooth, silky hair.

Reality came rushing back in the form of an open penthouse door. She was certain she'd closed and locked it before leaving.

"Pia?" she called.

When there was no answer, Serena entered with some trepidation. The floors had been vacuumed and the sofa's cushions plumped up. The maid had come by maybe.

That had to be it, and would certainly explain the polished dining room table, and the shiny appliances on the wet bar. The twin beds were made and the clothing she'd so hastily discarded hung up. But the dresser drawers were wide open, and the costume jewelry she'd left lying on top of the dresser looked like someone had gone through it.

A quick glance revealed nothing missing, not her expensive Hermès bag or her designer dresses, not the strappy Jimmy Choo shoes she'd paid a fortune for, or her new laptop.

Maybe Pia had come back, searched through the items, and left. But why would she leave the door open? Maybe the maid had gone off to get towels. Serena would speak to Pia first, and if she hadn't come back to the room, Serena would call Guest Relations and complain.

She had already wasted ten minutes and would have to hurry now. Quickly she slipped into a copper one-piece suit cut high on the thigh and pulled a sheer caftan over her head. Stepping into three inch copper-colored wedges, she found a towel and shoved her *Alexandra's Dream* card and the pendant into a bag. She added sunscreen, dark glasses, a hairbrush, notepad and pen.

Making sure the door was closed and locked, Serena skipped up the one flight of stairs to Artemis.

While she was looking forward to spending time with Marc, she couldn't help wondering what kind of sick game he was playing. He'd left her in Buenos Aires, feeling hurt, angry and confused.

Maybe she'd been wrong about him. Maybe he was the kind of man who came on to a woman, and once she became interested in him, backed off. Maybe he was a dandi, the South American version of player.

Marc was standing, a hand shading his eyes, as she stepped out on the deck. He wore aviator sunglasses, a T-shirt, and board shorts that came down to his knees.

Serena thought about another time when he'd been waiting for her.

They'd spent the day on her friend's yacht. Marc's skin had been the color of toast, his hair wet and slicked back off his face, his eyes shaded by dark glasses. He'd been waiting for her to come out of the stateroom they'd shared. She'd marveled at just how relaxed he'd become in such a short time. And when he'd seen her emerge from that room, his face had lit up like the sun.

"Just look at you," he'd said, coming toward her and taking her hands.

"I bet you say that to all the women," she'd flirted back.

Serena's memories were put on hold when Marc spotted her, waved. They met halfway, and when he kissed her she was even more certain this was Marc LeClair. The scent of Asian spice was not a smell you easily forgot.

They spent the next hour in The Mermaid Lagoon swimming laps and frolicking in the water. Afterward they decided to go in search of a drink.

At the bar they sipped rum and cokes and talked about why they'd decided to cruise. Marc claimed that he'd needed a long overdue vacation, so when he'd seen the dance charter advertised, he couldn't resist. He'd been taking ballroom dancing lessons in his leisure time.

The more they spoke, the more Serena was convinced that this was the man she'd spent two delightful weeks with in Buenos Aires. Why was he lying? What did he have to hide?

"I want to kiss you," Marc whispered in her ear.

"I want you to kiss me," Serena whispered back. "Where should we go?"

"My stateroom has a small veranda and I don't have a roommate. We could take our drinks there. No, forget I said that. It's really quite forward of me."

"Let's go," she said, coming to a decision. "Where's my purse?"

She was sure she'd put her rattan bag on the seat next to them. The seat was empty. She had a minimal amount of money in it, but she'd put the pendant in her purse before leaving.

"I have it," Marc said, holding the bag by the handles and giving it a little shake.

Marc held the purse as they took the two flights of stairs down to Hermes and his stateroom. He had to have paid a small fortune to have single accommodations. Although she and Pia could well afford it, they had balked at the 150 percent markup fee the cruise ship charged a sole occupant.

"Let me refresh your drink," Marc said when she was settled into an armchair.

"What I'd like is some water."

Marc handed her one of the bottles that had been sitting on the dresser. "Ice?"

"No, room temperature is fine."

He opened up the sliding glass doors that led to the veranda, letting in the humidity. When he stepped out onto the balcony he crooked a finger at her.

In seconds she was in his arms, and kissing him with a passion that she'd tried to keep under wraps for far too long. She savored the familiar taste of him.

Serena wrapped her arms around Marc's waist and let the kiss carry her away. She put her heart, soul and the six months of missing him into it. He was getting aroused and that excited her. Serena teased him with her tongue, using that same tongue to slowly explore his mouth. She pressed her damp body against his, and sensually rubbed her nipples against his chest.

"I'm not going to be able to put the brakes on if you continue to behave like this," Marc growled as his breathing grew ragged.

"Brakes? We are not driving a car."

He laughed against her mouth. "It's an expression. It means I won't be able to stop."

"Why would you want to stop? I am enjoying this and enjoying you."

She felt him go still, and wondered why the hesitancy. She'd just given him the go ahead. Most men would not need further encouragement.

Her body tingled with excitement and anticipation. She was on the brink of discovering whether he had lied or not. Once they made love she would know for sure. Marc hugged her close and rested his forehead against hers. She could feel the heat coming off his skin and feel his response.

"I want to sleep with you," he said. "I've thought of nothing else from the moment we met."

"I've been fantasizing, too," she answered boldly.

"Then we should go inside and spare the people of Key West and the boarding passengers a show."

Retracing their steps, Marc immediately pulled the curtains closed. Serena heard him rustling around getting out of his clothing. She quickly got naked.

He brought her into the circle of his arms, pressing his nude body against hers. When she took him into her hands, his erection came alive. He was breathing like a man who'd run miles.

Serena ran a hand over his bunched muscles. She got a whiff of that heavenly Asian spice. And when he kissed her again she practically inhaled him. She knew for sure she'd been with him before. They were in synchronization, matching each other move for move.

Marc's hands roamed her body, his fingers traced her collarbone, then wandered down to circle and tease a nipple. Serena's hands kneaded the tight flesh of Marc's buttocks. He turned her around so that she was seated on him, her back to his front.

He nipped at her shoulders and used his tongue to trace patterns on her back. She was pulsing all over, and guiding his hands and fingers to her feminine center, she ground herself against him. The friction turned the heat up another watt.

"I'm taking you to bed, baby," Marc said. And before Serena could answer he scooped her up.

She was on her back on his bed, her thighs parted. Marc reached for a packet in the wallet he'd left on the night stand. Using her mouth, Serena helped him slide the condom on. He fitted himself between her legs and entered her. Then the wild ride began.

Serena was panting, whimpering....

"Don't stop. Please don't stop."

"I have no intention of stopping, baby."

His lovemaking was just as she remembered. He did not need a manual or verbal instructions. He knew exactly what she liked and she knew exactly what turned him on.

Serena wrapped her legs around Marc's buttocks and simultaneously he brought her to a half-seated position. Seesawing back and forth, they stared into each other's eyes.

She hadn't been mistaken about his identity. This man was Marc LeClair. She knew his body almost as well as her own. She remembered the sounds of their lovemaking, even the slight hitch in their breath when they were minutes away from release.

Serena clutched Marc's shoulders as the first

shudder rippled through her. Sensing she was close to coming, he plunged into her, held tight and rode her hard.

"Serena, my Serena. You are much better in the flesh than any one of my fantasies."

Then his body went taut and she began to quiver.

She'd dreamed of this, had hoped to be loved by him again.

But good as it was, she didn't trust him.

CHAPTER TEN

ELIAS STAMOS'S GRUFF voice came through the earpiece.

"What the hell is going on, Nick? We haven't had one single voyage that's been uneventful. Now it looks as if an employee has jumped, or was thrown overboard. Reporters are calling me from all over the world."

"Security is on top of it and I am fully accountable," Nick said evenly. "I am confident it will get resolved."

Elias took a deep, centering breath, obviously having trouble holding on to his temper. "What do these security guards that were drugged say?"

"According to Sean they don't remember much of anything, other than a man approaching with questions."

"And it would be foolish to ask if they are able to describe this person?"

"Male. Dark hair. That's about as much as they remember."

"Crew or passenger?"

"They don't know."

Elias snorted. "What a worthless lot. That description could match almost any male aboard. This voyage must end on a positive note. I'm trusting you to find out who's behind this. Sadie and I will join the ship in Barbados to see Ariana get married, and when I do, I expect this situation to be over with and the passengers leaving happy."

"It will be resolved," Nick promised, although he didn't have a clue how to make this happen. Since early morning, Sean had been drilling away at the two security guards, to no avail. The men simply had no recollection of anything other than a man approaching them.

After Elias hung up, Nick stood thinking about it all, trying to come up with a plan of action. He wasn't sure how long he remained in quiet contemplation until Helena's voice broke through his haze.

"Honey," Helena called from the bedroom. "I gather my father is on the warpath and upset about this latest development."

"He has every reason to be upset. Bad press costs us money. Passengers are usually reluctant to book."

In tune with his moods, as she always was, Helena stood in the doorway, her arms crossed.

"You more than anyone should know his roar is far worse than his bite." She uncrossed her arms, bracelets jangling. The sound of those bracelets was music to Nick's ears. She was wearing his robe, which was much too big for her, and looked like the wide-eyed young woman he had first met years ago. She came to him and wrapped her arms around his middle, laying her head against his chest.

"You have a lot to think about, love. We'll see each other later, okay?"

She kissed him, giving it her all. Nick kissed her back with an unbridled passion. He counted on Helena to keep him centered and balanced. Being captain was a lonely business, and real friendships were few and far between. A huge responsibility lay on his shoulders, and he needed to make his decisions with authority and confidence. Too many people depended on him. This psycho, whoever he was, needed to be stopped.

Nick was prepared to do just about anything to get his ship back under control.

SERENA SAT OUTSIDE on the veranda in the darkness thinking about Marc and the intimate time they'd spent together. He'd made her feel special and cherished.

She heard movement from inside and shifted her body until she could see the penthouse's interior. She waited for her roommate to come out looking for her.

"Pia, is that you?" she called when her friend did not poke her head out.

"Sí, querida," Pia finally called back. "I am back from a wonderful day at the beach, and I am exhausted. Too much sun and too much to drink."

Serena rose from the teak chaise lounge and entered the suite through sliding glass doors. A very pink and freckled Pia stood barefoot gulping bottled water.

"Something's different about you," Pia greeted her, setting down the bottle she was chugging from. "You're dreamy and distracted, as if you are in love. It must have been some day."

"The best. I was with Marc. I am now convinced he is lying."

"You made love to him, hmm."

It was a statement, not a question, and did not require answering.

Pia set down the bottle and stretched both arms over head.

"Okay, don't answer. I am going to try to get some sleep before the dance this evening. Those things tend to go on forever and we will be forced to sit through a drawn-out dinner."

"I may do the same," Serena said, yawning, sleep deprivation from the evening before catching up with her. "By the way, we should be more careful when we leave the suite. I came back earlier to get something and the door was wide open."

"It was? I'm sure I closed and locked it before I left. I jiggled the handle several times just to be sure."

"Maybe it was the maid or butler. There were dresser drawers wide open and my costume jewelry looked like it had been gone through. I assumed you needed something to match what you were wearing."

Pia flopped onto her bed and stretched out. "That wasn't me," she said, yawning again. "Maybe we should say something to the front desk about this. How's your neck? Is it better?" She bolted upright.

"Where's the pendant, Serena? Have you checked to make sure it wasn't taken?"

"It's still in my purse, I think."

"Look, please."

Serena found her purse and removed the velvet pouch. "Here it is."

"Oh, good. At least it's not gone. Don't let me oversleep."

"I'll set the alarm."

Serena did that, slipped under the covers, and closed her eyes, thinking about Marc. A warm, wonderful feeling came over her. Marc LeClair's lovemaking had been out of this world. He knew how to make her feel good.

The next time they made love—and there would be a next time—she was going to make sure that she saw every inch of his magnificent body. None of this pulling the shades, and turning off the light.

They would be outdoors, and if she couldn't swing that, then she would insist that the lights be kept on.

TRACY HAD JUST MADE IT through another trying rehearsal with Janice, the dance captain. The woman had pushed them hard and the balls of Tracy's feet ached. Every muscle was stretched to its limit.

Pacing the confines of her cabin, she waited for the phone call from her son. She'd only been able to speak to Franco about once a week. There was no set time or day.

Sal doled out those calls as he'd doled out his affection during their brief marriage. She had no idea where he was holding her son, but she hoped he was safe. As a result, most of her free time was spent in her cabin, waiting next to the phone.

She was really beginning to hate her ex-husband. Well, maybe hate was too strong a word. She despised him. He was pathetic, but so was she. She'd fallen for a fast-talking player she thought could save her. Sal had promised her the world.

When the phone rang, she eagerly reached for the receiver. *Please God, let it be her son.*

"Hello, Franco, is that you, baby?"

A guttural laugh filled her ear. "*Prego,* not Franco, not yet. I need you to take care of something for me."

What now?

"What is it, Sal? I've already told you who has the pendant."

"That might be so, but I still don't have it. The idiot cabin steward who was supposed to get it for me botched the job. He screwed up like you, but he won't screw up again."

More raucous laughter followed. Goosebumps rose on Tracey's arms. She'd heard about the newly hired steward who'd jumped overboard or been pushed. She'd known Sal was cruel, but she'd never thought he would murder anyone. *And he had their son.*

Tracy wanted to ask him the truth about what had happened to Milutin Krupinsky. But did she really want to know?

"*Bella,* are you there?"

"Yes, Sal, I'm listening."

She wanted to spit, he disgusted her so.

"Then hear this. You are to make friends with Serena d'Andrea and her roommate. You are to report back to me and let me know their every move. I want to know everything—where they're going, and when they return to their suite. No movement is too trivial to report. Encourage the d'Andrea woman to leave the pendant behind in her suite for safekeeping. Tell her she is putting her life at risk by wearing it out. *Capisce?*"

"Why would she believe me?"

"It is your job to convince her of that. Make friends with the women and get them to invite you to their suite. You'll then have access to the pendant."

The goose bumps on Tracy's arms multiplied.

"Sal, I would get fired. I'm not allowed to visit passenger cabins. You know that."

"Rules are made to be broken, *bella*. You make friends with the women, then you make them trust you, and you steal the pendant. Simple as that."

"Let me speak to my son right now," Tracy demanded in an unusually forceful move. "I am not renewing my contract after this voyage. I'm returning to Las Vegas and my old show girl job. I want my son home."

Another cruel chuckle followed.

"You'll have the whining little brat as soon as you deliver the goods. I no longer have a partner so I have to depend on you. We're on a three-party call. Franco is on the other end of the line, holding for you. Shall I put him through?"

"Please."

Tracy would grovel if that's what it took to talk to her son. Sal was an insensitive swine and she hoped he'd had the common sense to keep Franco on mute. He shouldn't have to listen to the way his father spoke to his mother.

"Baby are you there?"

"Yes, Mommy. I miss you. When are you coming to see me?" He started to cry and it almost broke Tracy's heart.

"Soon, baby boy, soon."

Franco's adorable lisp filled her ear, but it was his tears that got to her. She loved this child more than life itself, and she would do anything to get her son back.

"I want to come home. When are you coming?" Franco pleaded, his voice wavering.

"Soon, baby, soon. Remember Mommy loves you."

Sal's voice broke in. "Say goodbye to your mother, boy."

"Bye, Mommy, I love you." Franco ended on a heart-wrenching sob.

The call disconnected and Tracy bit down on her bottom lip, almost drawing blood. The receiver dangled from its cord as she fell to the floor in a crumpled heap.

Sal would get his, she swore. If it was the last thing she did, she would make him regret his cruelty.

"THERE YOU ARE. I was beginning to think you wouldn't show," Heddy said, bearing down on Marc.

"Hi, Heddy."

Marc managed a nod and a smile in the woman's direction. He didn't want to hurt her feelings, but she was becoming something of a nuisance, constantly seeking him out.

Until then he'd been perfectly content to stand on the sidelines, admiring the competitive dancers, especially the women in their colorful dresses as they floated around the deck, their partners showcasing them.

"Are you competing in any heats?" Heddy asked.

"No, I don't think so. I much prefer looking. What a perfect night this is," Marc added, quickly changing the subject when Heddy continued to stand next to him.

He pointed to the open roof and the crescent-shaped moon up above. Stars sparkled like strewn diamonds against a velvety sky. It was a night made for romance, but not with this woman.

His thoughts shifted to Serena. Making love to her had reinforced what he had known all along. They were a perfect fit on so many different levels. All he wanted to do now was hold her again and smell the clean fresh scent of her hair.

Heddy's whispered words brought him back to the present.

"Yes, there's nothing more romantic than being out on a cruise ship and dancing under the stars. I was hoping you'd be my partner in the rhythm dancing heat."

The plunging neckline of her gold dress gaped as

her breasts grazed his arm. Marc took a couple of steps back, placing a decent distance between them.

"Uh, Heddy…"

She pouted. "You told me you came on this cruise alone."

"I did."

"So then why don't we hook up? We're both single and available."

Before he could say a word, Heddy took his arm, moving him onto the dance floor. She struck a pose and began a seductive Argentine tango.

Like a predatory cat, she strutted toward him. She had a gleam in her eye, and her hands stroked her body invitingly.

Marc reluctantly began *La Caminata*—The Walk— but his head was not into it. He moved forward on the balls of his feet and could almost hear Heddy counting the beat in her head. *One,* two, *three,* four, the emphasis on the first and third beats.

She was a by-the-book dancer and mechanical to boot, but her appearance drew a lot of attention. When men looked at her they thought about sex. But Marc was not interested. He liked women who were less obvious about their sexuality, who were open, charming and playful. Women like Serena, whom he wished he was dancing with now. She was the one who turned him on, not this woman.

It was Serena he kept in mind as he placed his right hand on Heddy's back and brought her cheek to cheek. He stared over Heddy's shoulder straight at his fantasy.

Serena's stricken expression told him what she was thinking. Marc wanted to race off the floor and go to her. He wanted to explain that he'd been the one pulled onto the dance floor, and that there was nothing between him and Heddy.

Releasing Heddy, Marc took a backward step. His partner, knowing she had the crowd's attention, did a Zarandeo—a little shake, twisting her upper body slightly to the left, then right again, and then returning to the straight ahead position. What a show-off she was, a definite tease.

Marc was left with no choice but to continue dancing. When he looked in Serena's direction again, she'd disappeared.

CHAPTER ELEVEN

SEEING MARC DANCING so intimately with another woman shook Serena more than she was willing to admit. They'd just made love and she was feeling both elated and vulnerable. Would he pull the same antics that he'd done before? There weren't that many places to hide on a cruise ship, but what if he was out for a little fun and she had just been convenient?

Serena took a deep breath and sipped on a glass of water. She'd almost convinced herself she didn't care who Marc danced with, and therefore had no reason to feel possessive, when she caught a glimpse of him and Heddy sailing by. The brazen woman had all her assets on display and all eyes were on the two of them as she shook and jiggled every ounce of her flesh.

Maybe she'd been taken in by a player, Serena thought, and not for the first time either. Eventually she would get it through her head that Marc was one of those smooth talkers good at getting a woman out of her panties in minutes.

"*Querida,* it's just a dance—one stinking little

dance, no big deal," Pia hastened to assure her. "That woman is a predator."

"If you say so, but I find it highly insulting he has no interest in rhythm dancing with me, but he carries on with her." Serena threw her hands in the air and made a clicking sound with her tongue.

"You *are* jealous."

"I am not."

Pia took Serena's arm and steered her in the direction of one of the poolside bars. "We will get drinks, and you and I will find dance partners. We will have a good time, I promise. When you have calmed down, maybe you can have a conversation with Marc."

They got drinks and returned to find another heat in progress. Dancers at the bronze level who wanted to compete in the Smooth Dance heat were on the floor warming up. Others who wanted to dance for the sheer pleasure of it were invited to join them.

The tune was a favorite, and Serena's shoulders dipped and swayed in time to the music.

"May I have the pleasure?" a deep voice asked from behind her. Recognizing Thanasi Kaldis, Serena spun around, flashing him a bright smile.

"I would be delighted."

The hotel director looked tanned, fit and especially handsome in his dress whites and stripes. He was accompanied by Andreas Zonis, who already had Pia by the hand.

"Red suits you," Thanasi said graciously, referring to the strapless dress with the billowing skirt Serena was wearing. "And the pendant is the perfect choice to wear with that outfit. Does your neck no longer hurt?"

"The ache is gone," Serena admitted, touching the bruised spot and laughing lightly. "And thank you for the lovely compliment. Now that I don't have to worry about, how you say, getting mugged again, I thought I'd wear the piece and see what kind of perks I can get. That man who attacked me is no longer around, right?"

"You need not worry," Thanasi assured her. He seemed somewhat distracted and kept scanning the crowd as if looking for someone. The music changed and more people came onto the dance floor. Serena looked around, hoping to spot Marc and his sexy partner. She wanted him to see that she was perfectly capable of attracting her own dance partner, and an accomplished one at that.

To Serena's relief, Heddy was now being escorted onto the floor by Sal Morena. They made the perfect pair. But Serena's smile slipped a watt when the couple slid into a spot next to them. Where was Marc, she wondered?

And although Sal's attention seemed to be focused on his partner, he still managed to mouth, "Lady in red, you are *bellisima*."

Heddy's reaction was to stretch her lips into an imitation of a smile and jiggle her chest. She regained Sal's attention almost immediately.

Serena tried to concentrate on the music and her own dance partner.

The hotel director placed his left hand between Serena's shoulder blades and waited for the host to officially begin the dance.

Serena, who'd always loved a good Viennese waltz, was now determined to live in the moment. Thanasi was an expert leader and they floated on the balls of their feet, circling the room. As he expertly turned her, she spotted Patti Kennedy amongst the onlookers.

The cruise director did not look at all pleased to see them dancing together. Her pained grimace probably had something to do with the wicked crush she was trying her best to hide. How did Thanasi not see Patti was in love with him? Or maybe he did, and planned to do nothing about it?

Serena's thoughts returned to Marc. When they'd parted earlier he'd said they'd meet here. He must have said the same thing to Heddy. Was he juggling them both?

The tune ended, and Thanasi, the perfect gentleman, bowed over Serena's hand. He returned her to the spot where they'd first met. Pia and Andreas were already off the floor and in a corner conversing as if they were the only two who existed.

Serena was feeling abandoned and used, just as she had six months ago when she'd first made the mistake of becoming involved with Marc.

"Did you manage to get any sleep?" a male voice asked. She turned to see Marc, who was dressed in black tonight, holding two wineglasses. He smiled down at her and handed her one. "Red suits you," he said.

"Thanks, yes, I did. How about you?"

"I was out like a light, dreaming wonderful dreams of being seduced by an exotic Argentine woman."

"Anyone I know?" Serena countered playfully, though inside she still seethed. What was he trying to do? "My recollection was that it was the other way around. You invited me to your stateroom."

Marc clinked his wineglass against hers. "You are utterly delightful. A breath of fresh air."

She wondered if he'd said much the same to Heddy. Serena didn't trust Marc but couldn't ignore the chemistry she felt between them—a wicked one at that.

The music picked up again, and the host on the raised dais announced the heat for Latin Dancing would soon begin. Participants were asked to sign in and pick up their numbers.

Excited contestants now swarmed the floor, feet tapping, fingers popping, heads bobbing.

"Come on," Marc said, taking Serena's wine goblet and setting it down on a table that badly needed bussing. "This is going to be fun."

Her jaw dropped, but she quickly clamped it shut.

"You don't mind rhythm dancing?"

Marc already had her by the elbow, and was easing her toward the place where they were to pick up their numbers. She pinned the card with the number on his back and he whisked her onto the floor.

They were warming up, practicing inside and

outside underarm turns, when Sal Morena and a new partner came onto the floor. Again he found a spot right next to her.

"The pendant doesn't do you justice," Sal said, almost leering at her despite the woman next to him. "Have you met my friend Tracy? She's a dancer on board." He stabbed a manicured finger in Serena's direction. "If you have the time she can tell you stories about the other women who found the pendant and their onboard romances."

"Perhaps some other time." Under her breath Serena whispered to Marc, "Can we find another spot to dance?"

"Sure."

Sal's dance partner, an attractive brunette with a vacant, unhappy smile, looked as if she was used to suppressing her emotions and enduring whatever came her way. Right now she seemed to want to get away from the man twirling her around. She had Serena's sympathies.

Marc meanwhile was getting into Glenn Miller. He was rock stepping and alternately slapping his knees to "In the Mood." He took Serena's hands and in a couple of deft movements jitterbugged her to a spot that was less crowded and away from Sal.

Serena allowed the mood and music to carry her away. She loved dancing with Marc, and it showed in her easy, confident steps. They were one of the top twelve semifinalists picked.

The dancing stopped while a buffet dinner was served poolside at the Mermaid Lagoon.

"I say we go to a smaller restaurant like the Olive Grove," Marc suggested. "It's bound to be less crowded."

"Okay, but I need to make a quick stop at my suite and change shoes. I'll meet you on Bacchus in ten minutes."

"Okay. I'll see if I can get us reservations."

They headed off in opposite directions.

As Serena walked down the long hallway, she again had the eerie feeling of being followed. It was ridiculous, because most passengers were either watching the shows or patronizing the clubs. She quickened her step and shot a look over her shoulder. There was no one behind her.

At her door, she rummaged through her purse looking for her key. A hand clamped over her mouth, and she was dragged backward.

"Ooomph!"

The man's free hand clenched her waist while the other remained over her mouth. He had her off her feet and began pulling her along. Serena kicked out and tried to bite the palm that was almost smothering her. Her efforts were to no avail and she was having a hard time breathing.

Laughter came from somewhere down the hallway, followed by raised voices. People were beginning to return to their staterooms. Serena renewed her efforts, kicking out again. She nipped at the man's palm and he froze, as if debating his options.

When he set her down abruptly, she pitched forward, losing her footing. In an attempt to break her fall Serena's arms shot out. Feet thudded past her. The man sped away, heading in the opposite direction.

"Hey, hey, take it easy," a woman called. "What's the rush? Is it some kind of costume ball? Why are you wearing a mask?"

"Oh, my God, that woman's been attacked!" another voice cried. "Help somebody! Help!"

More screams. More excited conversation.

Gentle hands holding hers; a voice she recognized as her friend's in her ear, "Serena, *querida*. Are you all right?"

"No, I'm not," she said, staring blankly.

Serena didn't remember being taken to the infirmary or being examined by the doctor. She didn't recall the sedative he prescribed, a sedative she didn't plan on taking. She didn't remember being put to bed by her roommate, either.

What she did recall was having a particularly vivid dream where she was held by Marc, who'd somehow magically appeared in her suite. He was swearing revenge on the man who'd done this to her.

She closed her eyes and laid her head on his shoulder and he hugged her tight. Between nods, she remembered tomorrow was a sea day, a good day to take it easy. She would go to the library and start writing that book.

She drifted to sleep remembering she was supposed to be somewhere, except she didn't feel much like moving. That's right. She was to have met Marc for dinner.

"Marc's waiting for me in The Olive Grove," she muttered, drifting off.

"No, he's right here," Pia said. "I sent someone to find him when you when you didn't show up."

"I told you he was wonderful." Serena let out a soft snore.

THANASI WAS in the officers' dining room when his beeper went off. He sighed loudly as he checked the incoming number. Patti sat across from him.

"It's Sean," Thanasi announced. "I guess I'd better find out what he wants."

He removed his radio from its clip and spoke into it.

"Come in, Sean. Sean, come in!"

There was the usual crackle and then Sean's voice came over the static.

"Thanasi you're needed on Zeus on the double. I'll meet you there."

"I'm on my way."

"Trouble?" Patti asked as he stood. "I can come with you if you like."

"No, finish your dinner. I'll beep you if I need backup."

And with that he hightailed it out of there.

A small group of passengers stood in the hallway conversing as Thanasi got off the elevator. He recognized most of them as the occupants of the four penthouses on that deck. Helena Stamos was amongst them. Two security guards were asking questions and taking notes.

Thanasi nodded to Helena and she acknowledged his greeting. There was no sign of Nick.

Sean, looking grim, exited from one of the penthouses. With a slight tilt of his head he gestured Thanasi toward the end of the hall.

"What's going on?" Thanasi asked when they were out of earshot of the passengers.

"That Argentine woman, the one who found the pendant—she was attacked as she was heading back to her suite."

"Is she hurt?"

"More like shaken up. From what I can piece together, she was returning to her room to change shoes. She'd agreed to have dinner with some guy she'd been dancing with. She was looking for her key when this guy grabs her and swings her off her feet. He clamps his hand over her mouth and drags her down the hallway. Then he must have heard people coming, so he releases her, she falls, and he scoots away."

"Anyone get a good look at him?"

"Her roommate says he was wearing a mask."

"Anyone else notice anything?"

"Only that he was tall and medium build. He was wearing black and the mask covered his head."

"Not much to go on, then."

"No, and the d'Andrea woman didn't see him because he came up behind her."

"As I recall she was wearing the pendant this evening," Thanasi said thoughtfully. "That must be the reason she's being attacked. Something's going on with that pendant."

Sean nodded, "I'd say so. She still has it in her possession. Maybe we should ask her to return it."

"What about this man she was supposed to have dinner with? Anyone question him? He obviously knew she was going back to her room."

"Actually, he's in the suite with the roommate. After Pia Fischer called us, she asked one of the passengers to find him in the Olive Grove, where he and Serena were supposed to meet, and bring him down. He's very angry."

"Hmm. Does Nick know about this latest development?" Thanasi asked.

"I suspect he's heard from Helena. I was leaving it up to you to tell him officially."

"I'll talk to Nick after I check on the ladies." Thanasi prepared to push off. "See what you can do about dispersing this group in the hallway. Maybe have the food and beverage director send each suite a bottle of wine and some hors d'oeuvres. Nick is going to have to contact headquarters and request additional security. Effective immediately we'll need all of your guards working around the clock. We need people stationed in each hallway."

"I already have someone reviewing the videotapes from the security camera in the hallway."

"Good." Thanasi squeezed Sean's shoulder before turning away. "Let me know what you find."

CHAPTER TWELVE

"HOW ARE YOU FEELING this morning?" Pia asked Serena, handing her a steaming cup of coffee.

Serena drew her knees up to her chest and pulled the covers around her. "Much better than last evening, and much more hopeful. Thanks for taking such good care of me."

"We take care of each other. Always have and always will. Why do you say hopeful?"

"Because things can only get better, right?"

"I love your positive thinking. It's still downright scary, though. I mean, you were attacked, and whoever attacked you is still on the loose."

"Yes, I know, but I have to hope that the tapes from the security camera will turn up something."

Pia was dressed in her workout clothing and was probably heading for the gym. She nibbled on a square of toast as she sat on the foot of the bed.

"Are you going to the kickboxing class or working out on the machines?" Serena asked, changing the subject.

"It's the treadmill for me today. I'll do my usual two miles."

"Maybe I'll join you."

Pia reached over to touch Serena's shoulder. "Are you sure you're up to it? It's a sea day. You could sleep in and do absolutely nothing."

But Serena's feet were already on the plush carpeting. She shoved a shank of hair out of one eye and stretched.

"I need to get out and about. I can't let some thug prevent me from enjoying every minute of this cruise."

"What a trouper you are."

Taking her coffee cup with her, Serena walked into the bathroom. Sunlight drifted in through the skylight above. The day was already shaping up to be picture perfect.

An hour later after an exhilarating workout, both women returned to the penthouse.

"Feels strange having security stationed on each deck as you get off the elevator," Serena muttered.

"But at least the cruise line is taking your attack seriously and precautions are being put in place. This is a good thing."

"I suppose. What are you going to do with yourself for the rest of the day?" Serena asked Pia, who was now going through her dresser drawers, muttering and dismissing one choice after another.

"I am going to sit around the pool, drink myself silly, and get brown as a berry. Later if I feel up to it I will try to get a private dance lesson from one of the pros. Maybe I'll finally learn how to foxtrot. What about you?"

"I'm going to take my laptop into the library and

I am not leaving until I have written the outline of my story."

"Good for you. No plans to see Marc today?"

"We didn't make any that I remember."

"Yes, you did. When he left last evening you said you would see him today."

Serena frowned. "I don't recall this conversation."

"Do you recall him coming to the penthouse last evening? You were supposed to meet up for dinner. He waited and waited and then finally I sent someone to find him. He was so worried he practically overstayed his welcome. I had to ask him to leave."

"I thought it was all a dream," Serena admitted, gathering up her laptop, a notebook, and a fistful of pens. "I'll look for Marc later and thank him. Have a good time whatever you do."

She marched out, heading for Bacchus, where the library was located. After a tough workout, coffee and a bite of toast was not about to hold her. On the way, she stopped off at The Rose Petal, where a late breakfast was being served.

Serena grabbed a quick cup of coffee, gobbled a bowl of fresh fruit and ate a scone. After stopping to admire the portrait of Alexandra Rhys-Williams Stamos, the owner's late wife, she continued onto the library.

Only a handful of people were in the room. Perfect. What she needed right now was peace and quiet, someplace where she could concentrate and put her thoughts in order.

A couple sat next to a picture window playing a

board game and talking quietly. A younger man was sprawled on one of the couches, nodding over a large book. And a silver-haired senior held a stack of books in one hand while chatting with the librarian, a woman with wavy dark hair and startling blue eyes hidden behind owl-like glasses.

Serena found one of the window seats and made herself comfortable. Here she could remain hidden and at the same time get a good view of the ocean rushing by. She did not want to think about last night's attack and why she was being targeted. She thought it might have to do with the pendant. Maybe she should just give it back. But that would be the coward's way out. And why would someone be so desperate to get it? It didn't make sense.

She patted the pocket of her linen Capri pants, making sure the jewelry in its velvet pouch was still there, then opened up her laptop, preparing to work. Next she dug the pamphlet from out of her purse and reread the legend of the tragic lovers.

If she punched up the storyline and made it more current, it would definitely appeal to young adults. Readers just adored star-crossed lovers. *Romeo and Juliet* still held the interest of young and old alike. It was a classic.

Serena was in the middle of jotting down her thoughts when in walked Patti Kennedy. Today she was dressed in shorts, T-shirt and a baseball cap. She must be on a day off. Patti pulled up a seat across from the librarian, whose name tag read "Ariana." Serena hunkered further into her seat. She could still get a good view of the women and unashamedly eavesdrop on their conversation.

"So when exactly is Dante joining us?" Serena heard Patti ask the librarian.

"A day or so before the shipboard wedding. He'll probably get on in Dominica."

"That's cutting it close. Aren't you the least bit nervous he might actually miss the wedding?"

"Sure I am, but getting the Italian authorities to give him the time off for two wedding ceremonies wasn't easy, especially after the Christmas holiday season when everyone was off. Dante had to use his contacts and his mentor had to pull strings. I'm just happy that he's humoring me with both a shipboard ceremony and the one back home in Philly."

"You're marrying a quality guy. Most men are nervous about one wedding ceremony, never mind two."

"Dante is simply the best. That's why I'm crazy about him."

Ariana removed her glasses and set them on the desk before her.

"How's the seduction of Thanasi going?" Ariana asked impishly, "I've noticed you guys have had dinner together a time or two."

Patti laughed nervously. "I don't think Thanasi sees me as a woman. He's respectful and kind but that's about it. He's eased up on the formalities now that I've proven I can do the cruise director's job as well as any man. I think he's interested in one of the women on board."

Ariana placed a hand over her mouth, smothering her laughter. "You are kidding, right? I can't imagine Thanasi being taken with a passenger. Not our anal, hardworking hotel director, the perfect company man. No way would he risk his position to indulge in a frivolous fling."

"What if it's not frivolous? This is the first time I've seen him dance with a passenger. And he's been dancing with this woman plenty."

Serena realized she'd been right on. Patti had a thing for the hotel director and that explained the accusing looks she'd been getting. It was uncomfortable hearing herself discussed but she was glad to have her instincts about Patti and Thanasi confirmed.

And Patti was way off base about Thanasi being interested in her. He had been polite and just doing his job. Beyond that he'd given no indication of wanting to get to know her on a personal level.

"What is this woman like?" Ariana asked, lowering her voice.

"Argentinean, exotic, charming, wealthy. When she bats those lashes, boy, does he come running. I can't hope to compete."

"Nonsense. You've got the looks, personality, and you two have something in common. You know what living aboard ship is like. Thanasi respects you and thinks you're smart. Here's what I would do."

"I'm all ears."

"You've got to take charge, but at the same time make him think it's his idea to pursue you, and that he's calling the shots."

Patti gasped loudly. "I'm supposed to play games and that will attract him?"

"A woman's gotta do what a woman's gotta do."

The two women laughed before Patti shot to her feet. "Gotta run, hon. I have an eleven o'clock massage. I don't want to be late. You'll let me know at some point what your maid of honor is supposed to wear."

"We'll go shopping together in St. Maarten."

"You're on. See you later."

Patti loped off, and Serena went back to writing the outline for her book. She would be careful from now on when she was around the hotel director.

The Kennedy woman had nothing to worry about. Serena's interest lay elsewhere—with the man she'd fallen in love with six months ago.

MARC READ THE E-MAIL several times. Santos Guerrera, the drug lord who'd threatened his life, was missing. It was suspected that he'd fled Colombia.

The other passengers seated in the Internet Café continued typing away, unaware of the impact this news had on Marc.

Call him paranoid, but he had a feeling that Santos or one of his henchmen was on board and sending him a not so subtle message through Serena. Someone must have found out about their relationship and was trying to get to him through her.

It wasn't that farfetched a thought. For months there had been threats on Marc's life, and once he'd narrowly escaped being run off the road. The thugs had even threatened to kidnap his daughter, whom his ex-wife had custody of.

Marc's boss was now suggesting he extend his vacation. He'd ordered him in no uncertain terms not to return to Colombia after the cruise ended. This might mean spending months away from the diplomatic career he enjoyed.

Marc typed a quick response and went off to find Serena.

She was sitting on the promenade sipping an espresso and looking contemplative when he caught up to her. There was a notebook on the table in front of her.

"Hi," Marc said, trailing a finger on her bare arm. "I didn't expect to find you out and about this early."

Serena set down her cup and gave him a beaming smile. "Do you think I'm about to let some lunatic confine me to my quarters? Besides, the hotel director has promised to increase security, so I'm feeling brave."

"When did he tell you that?" Marc asked, glad that they were taking the incidents seriously, but unhappy about the amount of contact Serena was having with the senior crew member.

"Thanasi called me this morning."

Marc didn't like the sound of that. He knew the man had a job to do, but his interest in Serena seemed to go beyond duty.

"What you need is a personal bodyguard and I know just the man for the job," Marc said, again trailing his fingers down her arm.

"And who would that be?" she asked, flirting right back.

"Me."

"You?"

He loved the way she smiled and tossed her hair out of her eyes. The chemistry between them was there on so many levels.

Marc pointed to the book she'd been scribbling in. "What are you doing, writing a journal?"

"No. Outlining the story I'm going to write."

"How about I get us both espressos and you can tell me all about the plot."

Without waiting for her answer, he wandered over to the espresso bar and waited for the attendant to pour them cups. All the while he could feel Serena watching him.

They talked about the book and the legend that had inspired Serena to write the story. Finally she left him midafternoon to attend an art auction, and Marc went off to the port lecture. The ship would stop briefly at Playa Carmen then on to Cozumel. He was anxious to hear about its history and the options for shore excursions.

Eventually he would have to tell Serena his real identity, though he knew she suspected the truth. But he would wait until Santos Guerrera was caught. Meanwhile he was going to stick to her side. If anyone was going to get hurt then it would be him.

CHAPTER THIRTEEN

THE NEXT DAY Pia invited Serena to join a group of people she'd met the evening before. They planned on taking the tender to Playa del Carmen, touring the ruins in Tulum, and then taking the ferry back to Cozumel where they would shop and sightsee.

"Where did you meet these people?" Serena asked as they stood in the lobby, the agreed meeting place.

"Last night they were at La Belle Epoque and we got to talking. Tracy Irvine's a dancer on board and she was with them. It's her day off and she volunteered to take us around. She seems pleasant enough, although a little unhappy. I feel sorry for her."

"Tracy? Why does that name sound familiar?"

Pia shrugged. "I don't know. But here she comes now."

Pia waved at a brunette who was hurrying toward them. There was something about her name and face that was familiar. It would come to Serena eventually.

"Hey," Tracy greeted Pia, "sorry I'm late." The two women exchanged kisses.

"This is my friend, Serena d'Andrea." Pia nudged Serena forward.

The entertainer stuck out a hand. "Hi, I'm Tracy Irvine, we met briefly a few evenings ago."

"Pia tells me you're a dancer."

"Yes, I am."

Although the woman smiled brightly, and her handshake was firm, she had a vacant expression in her eyes and a slight puffiness to her face as if she'd been crying.

Sal had been dancing with her the other evening. She was the one who'd looked as if she couldn't wait to get away.

"Who are we waiting for?" Serena asked, looking around the opulent lobby. A long line of people hoping to secure last minute shore excursion tickets swarmed the Guest Relations Desk.

"Ed and Alison. They're a couple from Los Angeles. Diego and Tim said they would be here as well. Diego you already met, Ted's on the charter too."

"That's seven total. Here come Alison and Ed now," Tracey said.

Serena watched a young couple with fanny packs belted around their waists approach. There were more kisses and the requisite introductions all around.

"And there's Diego and Tim getting off the elevator," Pia added.

"Good. We can grab the next tender," Tracy said.

They hurried down three flights of stairs and were lucky enough to catch the next boat.

On shore, the passengers followed the guides armed with yellow flags and boarded buses.

Diego chose the seat next to Serena. He draped an arm loosely around her shoulders. "How's the cruise going for you so far?" he asked. "You recovered nicely from that nasty incident when the pendant was ripped from your neck."

"I've tried not to think about it. I came aboard to have fun."

Diego must not have heard about the most recent attack and Serena decided not to tell him. She didn't want to put a damper on their outing.

Soon they were off, taking the winding roads that led to the Mayan ruins. On the way they passed several locals who stopped to wave at them. They'd been driving for almost twenty minutes when Alison said out loud, "I wonder how Tulum got its name?"

"I know," said Tim, the quietest of the lot. "It's because of the walls surrounding it."

"Give that man a prize," Diego joked.

"Originally it was called Zama, Place of the Dawning Sun," Tracy informed them, although she seemed a bit distracted.

Finally the ancient city in all its awesome glory stood before them. The turquoise ocean lapped at its base. It was one of the most breathtaking sights Serena had ever seen.

"It's hard to believe people lived here," Pia said.

Serena gazed at the graceful columns and elegant carvings, which were remarkably well preserved. "It is impressive."

For the next two hours they trudged along behind their guide, who spoke excellent English. He whisked them through the Temple of Frescoes, where they got to see the partially restored murals depicting the Mayan gods. After that they entered the Castillo Pyramid, which had served as a beacon or lighthouse. The Temple of the Diving God was next on their list.

"Imagine living here," Serena said, gazing up at the fortress.

Pia laughed. "It would be one expensive piece of real estate."

They had time to shop, then reboarded the buses and drove to the ferry that would take them to Cozumel, where the ship was docked. It was decided that Tracy, who knew the small island best, would be the one to play tour guide.

Tracy suggested they try the outdoor market once they'd reached Cozumel. She claimed it was the best place to buy silver and the papier mâché clowns Pia collected.

As they roamed through the winding alleyways, they were assaulted by cries of "Come in, madam. Very cheap, madam." Finally they found a vendor selling unique silver jewelry.

"Show the man your pendant and see if he'll barter with you," Pia said jokingly, "maybe exchanging it for another piece will change your luck."

"I can't do that," Serena protested. "It's the ship's property."

"Oh, come on," Pia urged her. "Show it to him and see what he says."

It must have been Serena's imagination, but Tracy appeared to brighten at the mention of the pendant.

"Do you have the piece with you?" she asked.

"Yes, in my purse."

"Why aren't you wearing it?"

"Well, there's no one around to give me perks," she joked. "But seriously, it's not the kind of jewelry you wear with casual clothes."

Diego had just paid for the onyx chess set he'd negotiated down to a third of the asking price. He came up behind Serena and pinched the nape of her neck. She found herself wishing that it was Marc doing that instead of him, and she wondered where he was today.

Alison and Ed were now looking at blankets. To pass the time, Serena began poking through a tray of earrings and cufflinks. She'd been thinking of picking up a couple of souvenirs for her parents.

"I thought you were going to show the pendant to the shopkeeper?" Tracy said, nudging her.

"I will."

Why was everyone so fixated on the pendant?

Serena dug through her purse, found the velvet pouch, and handed it to the shopkeeper.

"Can you tell me how much this is worth?"

The vendor nodded, then said, "No exchanges, though. You buy from me in American dollars."

"Of course."

Serena picked out a couple of items on his tray. Her mother might like the silver-and-onyx hat pin, and a belt buckle that looked antique would suit her father. With Diego's help, she was able to get the price down to something that was mutually acceptable.

Tracy was trying to move them along, tempting them with the prospect of Carlos and Charlie's. They hailed another taxi and headed for the popular bar. After going only a short distance, Serena realized she'd left the pendant with the vendor.

"Please stop," she shouted. "I've got to go back to the market."

The taxi driver braked sharply and his passengers pitched forward. Before the car came to a full stop, Serena raced from the vehicle. Diego was right behind her.

"Did you forget something?"

"Yes, my pendant."

They wove their way through the narrow alleyways, and after a couple of false twists and turns Serena found the booth where they'd made their purchases.

The shopkeeper seemed pleased they'd returned. "I knew you would come back to get those cufflinks."

"I'm back for my pendant."

"What pendant?"

Diego spoke up. "The lady handed you a silver pendant in a little velvet bag. You were going to tell her how much it was worth."

"Oh, that. I gave it to her friend. I told her it's worth about as much as my nicest pair of earrings."

"Which friend was this?" Serena asked.

"The pretty dark-haired woman."

It had to be Tracy. But why hadn't she said anything? She must have known that's why Serena had gone back to the market.

Diego grasped Serena's forearm. "Let's go back and see what Tracy has to say. She probably just forgot."

The taxi was still there, the meter running.

"Did you find whatever it was?" Pia asked as they scrambled into the back of the vehicle.

"I forgot the pendant. The shopkeeper says he gave it to you, Tracy."

"He never gave it to me." Tracy sounded genuinely puzzled.

"Maybe you should check the paper bag with the shawl you bought," Diego suggested.

Tracy ignored him. "Let's get going," she said to the driver.

"No, don't move," Serena said. "If the shopkeeper is lying, I'm calling the police."

Diego backed her up. "Serena is right. You need to check that bag."

"It's in the trunk," Tracy said. "But if you want to go to Carlos and Charlie's, we really need to get going." She sounded annoyed.

Ed fished a paper bag off the floor. "Is this what you're looking for?"

Tracy shrugged. "Maybe."

Inside was a black wool shawl with silver threads through it. "There's nothing else in here."

"I'm calling the police," Serena said firmly, preparing to spring from the vehicle.

"No, wait," Tracy surprised her by saying. "Let's do a thorough search. If the police get involved, we'll never make it to Carlos and Charlie's."

Everyone piled out of the vehicle. After carefully going through every paper bag and package with no luck, the group decided to head back to the market and try reasoning with the vendor before getting the police involved.

"Let's check the taxi one last time," Tracy suggested. "Just in case it's stuck under a seat."

She led the effort, getting down on her hands and knees and beginning to search.

"Wait! Wait! I think I see something," she said, retrieving the velvet pouch from under the front seat. "The shopkeeper was telling the truth after all." She handed the pouch to Serena.

The pendant was still inside and Serena voiced her relief.

An hour later they were standing inside the crowded bar looking at the people dancing on tables.

It was loud, wild, and many of the patrons had clearly had too much to drink. Tracy pointed out several cruise passengers. Serena graciously accepted the drink Diego handed her and settled in to watch the raucous and sometimes inappropriate behavior.

She was considering heading back to the ship when Pia whispered in her ear. "Isn't that Marc over there with that woman?"

"Where?"

Pia pointed to a spot in a corner. Sure enough, there was Marc with Heddy draped all over him.

They looked very much the couple and he seemed to be eating up the attention.

Serena's stomach lurched. It was painful to watch the two of them together. She'd thought that after sleeping with Marc, she had established a special bond with him. Clearly she was wrong.

"Don't let him get to you," Pia warned. "Pretend to have a good time even if it kills you. Now, put a smile on that lovely face of yours and act as if you're having a good time. There's nothing like a bit of healthy competition to get the male testosterone revving."

Smiling was the last thing Serena felt like doing, but Pia's advice was sound. Why should she let Marc's interest in another woman ruin her good time?

Diego, who must have overheard some of the conversation, clinked his glass against hers.

"Want to dance?" he asked.

"Sure."

And although Serena didn't feel much like dancing, she got out on the crowded floor and pretended she was having the time of her life.

CHAPTER FOURTEEN

"YOU STUPID BITCH. You had that pendant in your possession and you handed it back to that woman. Why?" Sal was furious.

"What else was I supposed to do?" Tracy cried. "She was going to call the police, but I have...ouch! Stop it!"

Sal had her by the hair and there was no place to go, no place to escape to. She was sorry she'd agreed to meet him on the topless deck behind the smoke-stack, especially this late at night. Who knew what he would do to her here?

"It would have been your word against the shop-keeper's, so what do you care?" Sal said, yanking on a shank of hair.

She cared deeply. She was tired of being a pawn in his sick game. She just wanted her child. Sal wasn't even giving her the opportunity to tell him what she'd come to tell him, that she had Serena's purse in her possession.

"I couldn't do that to the man," Tracy pleaded. "It would have been wrong. He would have ended up in jail and he was innocent."

"What an idiot you are," Sal said, tugging on her hair again.

"Ouch! You're hurting me."

"You chose a stranger over the son you claim to love. You must not want to see him again."

"I love my son. I want him back, Sal, and I'll do almost anything to have that happen. I hoped that Serena would have forgotten about the pendant until after the ship sailed, but she didn't. I had no choice but to give her back the piece when she asked. There were people with us. It wouldn't have looked good."

"You could have lied and told her the shopkeeper never gave it to you." Sal yanked on Tracy's hair, emphasizing his point.

Tracy couldn't stop herself from crying out, and that seemed to make Sal angrier. He pushed her away from him. "Stupid bitch!"

Tracy lost her footing and slid across the slick deck. The purse she'd been holding fell out of her hand, sliding in the opposite direction. Seconds before her head hit the floor and stars exploded before her eyes, she sobbed, "I have Serena's purse and I'm certain the pendant is in it."

"What's going on? Who's there?" a male voice called from the darkness. A ring of yellow light illuminated the area inches from where they stood.

Security, thank God! They couldn't have arrived at a better time.

Footsteps pounded as Sal raced off.

THANASI HAD BEEN SUMMONED to Nick's cabin, which meant only one thing. Elias must be looking for an update, some sign that they were on top of things. There was nothing new to report. The steward was still missing, and the man who'd attacked Serena d'Andrea still had not been caught.

Nick appeared on edge when Thanasi walked in. He was cracking his knuckles and pacing.

"What does Sean say?" Nick demanded. "By now he must have looked at those security tapes. Has the assailant been identified?"

"Unfortunately, no. The man wore a devil's mask. It was impossible to see his face."

Pop! Pop! Pop! Nick went at his knuckles again.

"This animal is still free, roaming my ship, and can strike again at any moment."

"Sean is certain that with the additional security onboard we will catch him the next time he attacks," Thanasi said.

"The next time? What if he does something much more serious than try to abduct a woman? He may have killed that cabin steward, and now he's targeted the d'Andrea woman. He needs to be stopped."

"And he will be stopped," Thanasi said with a confidence he didn't feel. "You'll have to trust us on this. By the time this cruise ends, whoever is behind this will be apprehended."

Nick sighed loudly. "They'd better be, or I might be forced into early retirement."

Thanasi could tell Nick meant every word. Elias was probably riding him like crazy. Thanasi was one of the few people Nick Pappas allowed to see his frailties. The two went back a long way.

The d'Andrea woman was an heiress and wealthy in her own right. She came from a powerful publishing family. Maybe the attacks were kidnap attempts.

"I'm counting on you and Sean to find out who is behind these incidents," Nick said. "I want that animal caught and I want my ship back."

Thanasi nodded, preparing to leave. "You have my word we'll find out who's behind this. You will have your ship back."

Those were famous last words. He had no clue how he was going to make good on his promise, but he planned on doing everything in his power to see the thug behind bars.

He needed to talk to Sean and come up with a plan. Later, he was meeting Patti for dinner and he was excited about it being just the two of them. He didn't want to think about what that meant. In less than a week they would both be on vacation. For that reason only, he felt he could bend his own personal rules.

When Thanasi finally caught up with Sean, the ship still hadn't sailed. As Acting Chief of Security, Sean had spent most of the day on the phone with headquarters, updating them on the latest situation. He'd also had to brief the back-up security force that management had flown in to Cancún, and who had joined them in Cozumel. And he'd taken another look at the security tapes. Now he was exhausted, angry and admittedly stumped.

"You look like hell," Thanasi greeted him as they sat across from each other in Sean's small office, which was hardly bigger than a file cabinet.

"You don't look so good yourself," his colleague shot back, glancing up from the folder in front of him. He took another gulp of his steaming cup of coffee.

"Anything new?" Thanasi asked.

Sean shrugged. "No. This is truly puzzling."

"What about the tape? Anything significant on it?"

"Not much there. The man was wearing all black and that devil's mask covered his head."

"So you've learned nothing new?"

He paused. "The attacker wore a ring that was familiar."

"In what way?"

Sean picked up his cup and again took a swallow. "It was a band of silver and gold stars."

"Like the Liberty Line logo, the insignia that's on our smokestack."

"Exactly."

"We should talk to Nick," Thanasi said, rising. "He's in constant contact with Mr. Stamos. Perhaps it would mean something to both of them."

"Okay, I'll come with you."

Thanasi hoped this wouldn't take forever. Patti would be waiting at the diner where they'd agreed to have a quick bite. The ship sailed later and she was hosting the midnight show.

They made a quick stop at Nick's quarters, but the

captain was either not in or not answering. Maybe he was having dinner in the dining room. But a stop in the Empire Room revealed his empty table.

Sean and Thanasi parted ways, promising to be in touch later. Thanasi headed off, a spring in his step at the thought of having dinner with Patti.

PATTI KENNEDY PRESSED her lips together, hoping the lipstick she'd recently applied didn't smudge. Thanasi was running late, but that was nothing new; one thing or another always came up. She was enjoying this time to herself and taking advantage of an almost empty ship. Any time alone was precious.

Most passengers had chosen to stay in Cozumel until right before the ship sailed. The few people back on board were at the buffet set up on Helios. As a result, the diner was almost empty. She and Thanasi could even pretend they were on a date.

"Ha!" she said out loud. Shipboard life did not allow for anything as civilized as dating. You hooked up or jumped right into a relationship, and in her position she couldn't afford either. When things got messy, there was nowhere to go. She'd worked much too hard to get where she was to lose it all by allowing her emotions to get in the way.

But Thanasi was different. He was an officer, a gentleman and technically her boss. He liked running a tight ship and didn't suffer fools easily. And he was well respected and one of the few people that she could learn something from.

But he was all about business; at least up until now

he'd always been. She wondered if he was more relaxed because it was the final voyage before their time off.

Like Thanasi, Patti was disembarking before the next cruise, a trip along the South American coast. Three months of vacation lay ahead, and although she had nothing planned, she couldn't wait. Going home to Lubbock, Texas, was not an option. She would only be harassed by her family, who would trot out every single male they knew in the hopes of getting her married. Maybe she would visit an ex-coworker in Australia.

"Are you saving that seat for someone, madam?"

Thanasi smiled widely. She'd never seen this playful side of him. What did you know, the ice was melting.

"Actually I'm saving the seat for my favorite hotel director," Patti flirted back.

"And who would that be?" he asked, sliding into the seat opposite her. "Have you ordered yet?"

"No, I was waiting for you."

Thanasi picked up the menu and began looking at it.

Recognizing him, a waitress hurried over.

"Are you ready to order, sir?"

Thanasi shook his head slightly. "Give us a minute."

Patti put her menu aside. "Seven days to go before this contract is over with and I can't wait."

"It's been a tough one. Every voyage has had its challenges. I'm beginning to think I'm too old for this kind of life."

"Me and you both. How old are you?"

"Forty-eight. And you?"

"Thirty-nine. Ancient." Patti chuckled. "Do you feel like sharing a pizza?"

"Sure, why not? Add a couple of salads and we're set."

The waitress returned and took the order.

As they waited, Patti looked around the deserted pool area.

"Feels good to have the ship almost to ourselves. It's times like these I wonder why I chose this crazy life. I value my privacy, and on a ship—" she waved her arms around "—no such thing exists."

"It's a fishbowl all right."

"When I was growing up in Lubbock, I had visions of being married with two kids by now. I wanted the house, white picket fence, a golden retriever slobbering all over the SUV's window, the whole bit."

"And you no longer want that?" He was looking at her closely, intently.

"Oh, I do. Don't you? But it's not like there's a long line of prospects." She sighed. The conversation had taken a strange turn.

"You could have any man you wanted," Thanasi said looking her directly in the eye, "But this business has become your man. You've made it your life."

He'd got her down pat. She'd buried herself in her work so that she didn't have to think. She'd driven herself mercilessly so that when she fell into bed at night she was too tired to reflect on how empty her life really was. They were very similar. Similar yet different. He kept a stiff upper lip and did what he had to do while she made light of things.

"Do you think I could really have any man I wanted?" she asked. This time she was the one who refused to break eye contact.

He smiled at her. "If you decide you want him, he's yours."

"What about you? Don't you miss having a woman in your life?" she asked softly.

"I miss the companionship, but I don't miss the fights or having to constantly answer to someone."

"Maybe she wasn't the right woman."

"Do we ever know if it's the right person?" Thanasi asked in a contemplative tone.

Patti tapped her chest. "We know in here."

He smiled. "You're a hopeless romantic. Where is that pizza?"

"Hopeful," Patti corrected. "Ever hopeful."

Their salads arrived and the pizza followed shortly after. As they ate they chatted about their crazy life on board.

While they were enjoying an after-dinner coffee, Thanasi's beeper vibrated. Patti noticed his guarded expression and realized he'd returned to officer mode.

"Something wrong?"

"It's Sean, which means there's trouble."

Patti was already on her feet. "Let's go."

"No, stay. You're still officially off."

"In our business there is no time off." Patti headed for the elevators and Thanasi quickly fell into step beside her.

Patti decided they were the perfect pair. Driven and overly committed.

CHAPTER FIFTEEN

"MY PURSE HAS BEEN STOLEN," Serena said to Kali, who was standing behind the Guest Relations Desk.

"Maybe you forgot it somewhere. I'll check the Lost and Found bin and see if someone turned it in." With a swish of dark hair she went off.

Serena didn't care for the employee's dismissive tones, but what could she do? Report her for being inattentive? That would be petty and Serena would come off like a diva.

She'd left Carlos and Charlie's shortly after seeing Marc and Heddy together. She'd felt sick to her stomach, and it had nothing to do with drinking. Tracy, claiming she needed to get back as well, had left with her. They'd taken a cab to the ship, and Serena was certain she'd had her purse with her then, because she'd paid the cab driver.

She had planned to go directly to her cabin and indulge in a little self-pity. She would order room service and sulk, or give herself a good talking-to. She'd come on a cruise to have fun, and she was not going to allow some lady's man to ruin her good time. From now on she was not going to take Marc

LeClair too seriously. She would play the same game he was and keep all her options open.

Somewhere between boarding and going to her suite, she had lost her purse. Serena mentally retraced her steps. Tracy had talked her into having a drink with her in the lobby bar.

Who had paid for that drink? Serena didn't remember. One drink had led to two. And although she wasn't that crazy about the woman, she'd ended up telling her more than she should about herself and Marc, her certainty that he was someone she knew, and that Gilles Anderson was not his real name.

"No man is worth losing sleep over," Tracy had said, that same vacant expression in her eyes. "Most are dogs. Out to get what they can, and that's that."

They were still seated at the bar when Diego, Pia and the rest of the group came charging across the lobby. They'd been having a good time at the tavern, and it showed. Serena had been persuaded to have yet another drink.

It wasn't until she was back in her suite and putting away the gifts she'd bought for her parents that she realized her clutch purse was nowhere to be found.

Serena had rushed around, tearing the place apart. She'd finally had to accept it was missing and had gone to the Guest Relations Desk. There hadn't been much money in the purse. She'd kept her credit card in the pocket of her shorts along with the ship card, but the passport she'd taken ashore was inside, and that was a problem.

Kali was back, her expression blank.

"Sorry, no purse has shown up. You may want to check back later." She shoved a form across the desk at Serena. "Fill this out. If someone turns in your purse we'll call you."

Serena filled out the paperwork and handed it back.

When she returned to her suite, Pia was getting dressed to go to the luau, and then a movie at the Starlight Theater.

"No, luck?"

Serena had told Pia about her missing purse at the bar.

"Unfortunately, no. I couldn't careless about the purse. It's my passport I'm most concerned about."

"It'll turn up," Pia said with a certainty Serena didn't feel. "Maybe someone picked it up by accident. Let's go to the luau and try to have fun."

"Thanks, but I think I'll pass. I've had too much to drink already and I'm not in the best of moods."

"Even more reason for you to get out of the suite. You'll just become more depressed if you sit here by yourself. What you need is a distraction."

But Serena had made up her mind. She stifled a yawn.

"You go and have fun. I'm going to bed."

"MISS, ARE YOU OKAY?" the security guard asked, shining his flashlight on the woman who was half-sitting up on the deck, hugging one knee.

"Just had the wind knocked out of me, that's all." She tried to smile brightly, but she must be hurt.

"I thought I heard someone arguing. You sure you're okay?"

"I'm fine."

She tried to stand but wobbled. He reached out a hand to steady her. "Maybe you should see a doctor."

"Not necessary. Where's my purse? I dropped it when I fell."

He shone his flashlight around the deck but there was no sign of a purse. The woman began crawling on her hands and knees, feeling under stacked lounge chairs and in crevices. Frustrated, she struggled to her feet again.

"Don't you have a brighter light?"

"No. This area is supposed to be off-limits after dark. I'll gladly escort you back to a public area."

"I know my way, thank you." She began hobbling away.

Her behavior was odd. Instead of being grateful to him for coming to her aid, she seemed anxious to leave. People were peculiar.

The guard shone his flashlight on the winding stairway, lighting her way, and watched her descend. Convinced she'd made it to the next deck, he continued his rounds. He'd gone maybe twenty feet when his toe hit an object and he almost tripped. Reaching down, he retrieved a flat rattan item shaped like an envelope. It was the purse the woman had lost.

His first thought was to go after her, but by now she could be anywhere. It occurred to him he didn't have a clue what her name was, and no way of getting the purse to her. He would take it to the Guest Relations Desk where Lost and Found was located.

But something about the encounter didn't sit right with him. He could swear the woman had been fighting with the man he'd seen run off, and that she'd made up the story about falling. He would turn the purse in to his boss, Sean Murphy, and let him handle it.

NICK WAS IN Sean's cubbyhole of an office when Thanasi entered. Patti had gone off to the luau to see if her assistant needed help hosting the event. They'd agreed to meet later after the midnight show.

"What's going on?" Thanasi asked.

"There's been an interesting situation."

"Interesting as in good or bad?"

Sean waved a straw bag at him. "One of the security guards found this."

"What is it?"

"A woman's purse."

"Finding a purse is hardly unusual," Thanasi said. "People leave their stuff behind all the time."

"It's not just any woman's purse," Nick interjected. "It belongs to the d'Andrea woman. She reported it missing and it was found on the topless deck. We opened it and verified the contents. A couple of souvenirs were found inside and her passport was still there."

"Okay, so she was on the topless deck, which isn't that unusual, and she left her purse behind."

"Sounds simple enough, but it isn't," Nick interjected, "Sean, perhaps you need to tell Thanasi the whole story."

Sean then dutifully repeated what the guard had told him.

"And we have no idea who this injured woman is, or who she might have been arguing with?"

"Not a clue. The guard assumed she was a passenger, so he didn't want to overstep his boundaries and ask for ID."

"Let's try calling the d'Andrea woman. We'll let her know we found her purse. Maybe she'll have some insight into what happened."

Nick handed the receiver to Sean.

"It's late," Sean reminded him, "I'd hate to wake her."

"If my passport were missing I wouldn't be able to sleep," Nick said firmly. "Get her on the phone."

Thanasi waited as Sean made the call.

"Ms. d'Andrea…Sean Brady, Acting Chief of Security here…yes, ma'am, your purse has been found. Will you be able to come down to the security office to claim it?" He listened for a moment. "Okay, go to Guest Relations and someone will bring you here. We'll see you in fifteen minutes." Sean hung up the receiver. "She's on her way."

"Why is it that this woman's been involved in every incident this cruise. She seems nice enough, but…"

"My job is to find out why she's being targeted," Sean interrupted. "You think the pendant has anything to do with it? We can have her hand it in."

Nick shook his head. "If she is a target, it's more likely to do with her family's wealth."

"Then maybe we should have insisted she come aboard with her own bodyguard."

"Too late now," Nick said. "While she's on this ship, she's our responsibility." He looked at Sean's empty coffee cup. "Can one of you gentlemen order us coffee while we wait?"

"I'll take care of it."

Thanasi unclipped his radio from his belt and spoke into it. "Food and Beverage come in, please. I need three espressos sent to the security office on the double. On second thought, make it four."

While they waited, Sean briefed them on the backgrounds of the new security men who had been flown in to join the ship.

"They're all retired law enforcement officers," he said. "Two of them will be undercover, mingling with passengers and trying to find out what's going on."

"It's good to have people on board that know what they're doing," Nick said as Sean visibly bristled.

There was a soft tap on the door.

"Come in," Sean called.

A head poked through the open door. "I have Ms. d'Andrea with me." It was Kali, one of the pursers. "She said I was to bring her here."

"We'll make sure Ms. d'Andrea gets back to her cabin safely," Sean said.

Kali entered the room with Serena. Serena's hair was mussed and she looked as if she'd hastily thrown on her clothing.

"You may return to your duties," Thanasi said to the purser, who was lingering. "Please have a seat, Serena." He held out a chair.

Another knock signaled the arrival of their espresso. Kali, reluctant to leave, finally edged out the door.

Sean waited until everyone had their cups in hand and the attendant left before addressing the situation.

"We're sorry to get you out of bed," Thanasi said to Serena.

"I wasn't asleep. Has my passport been found?"

Sean slid the purse in her direction. "Why don't you check for yourself?"

She opened the purse and dumped the contents on his desk. A compact, lipstick, small paper bag, a change purse, and a passport protected by a leather case came rolling out.

"Everything seems to be here," Serena announced.

"What about the pendant?" Sean asked carefully. "Did you take it into Cozumel with you?"

"Yes, I did. I had an incident in the market earlier, so I slipped it into my pocket for safekeeping."

The men exchanged looks.

"Where is the pendant now?" Sean asked.

"In the safe in my suite."

"When did you first notice your purse was missing?" Sean asked, scribbling away.

"When I got back on board."

"Who were you with in Cozumel?"

Serena named the people in the group.

"And Tracy, you say, is an employee."

"Yes, a dancer. She was the one who took us around."

"Can you describe her?"

Serena's eyebrows arched. She was probably trying to figure out where this was leading.

"Dark hair, dark eyes, pretty, nice figure. Maybe five foot seven or eight."

While she spoke, Sean continued his note taking.

"Do you have any enemies that you know of, Ms. d'Andrea?"

"Enemies?"

"People that don't like you or your family. Someone who might be holding a grudge."

"Not that I know of." Serena studied the three men. "Can I ask questions?"

"By all means," Nick said.

"Where was my purse found?"

Sean explained that a guard had turned it in.

"Strange. I've never been on the Topless Deck." Serena let out a shaky laugh. "I didn't know such a thing existed."

"You've never been there?" Nick repeated.

"No…never."

"I'm very concerned," Sean said. "We've increased security on board and we suggest you don't go anywhere unless you're accompanied by a friend."

Serena threw her hands in the air. "And there goes my freedom. If you've increased your security force and there's a man monitoring my deck, that should be enough."

"As you wish, Ms. d'Andrea," Nick said smoothly in an effort to settle her down. "The moment you feel you need additional protection, you are to contact Sean, understand?"

"I will. Now may I go?"

"Of course. The hotel director will escort you back to your cabin."

Serena slid her hand through the crook of Thanasi's arm.

Thanasi couldn't help thinking what an interesting woman Serena d'Andrea was, and gutsy as they came.

CHAPTER SIXTEEN

AFTER A RESTLESS night's sleep, and dreams of being chased by masked devils, an early-morning run was just what Serena needed. Another sea day lay ahead and she had no place to be until midafternoon.

Diego had promised to help her with her Hustle steps, and because it was formal night, she'd made an appointment to have her hair done. In between she planned to work on her book. Later that night, she and Marc were to compete in the Latin semifinals.

Serena had just completed her third lap on the running track when Marc caught up to her.

"Hey stranger," he greeted her.

"Hey yourself," Serena retorted. She refused to let on that his deep blue eyes and tanned body were turning her on.

"Where were you yesterday?" Marc asked.

"What do you mean?"

"I called you yesterday to ask you to go sightseeing with me in Cozumel, but no one answered."

Jogging in place, Serena tried to catch her breath. "I went to the ruins of Tulum with a group of people. We ended the day at Carlos and Charlie's."

Marc didn't flinch. He reached over and swept a lock of hair out of her eyes. She steeled herself not to respond to his touch.

"You push yourself really hard, don't you?"

It was an intimate gesture. Refusing to be a push-over, she kept jogging in place and didn't answer.

Marc held her by the elbow.

"How about we get together later and practice our dance steps. Maybe we could play a little Ping-Pong afterward."

"It's formal night," Serena reminded him. "I have a hair appointment."

"How about in a couple of hours?"

"I may be asleep or working on my book."

Marc gave her arm a little squeeze. "What's really going on, Serena?"

She took a deep breath. She had no claim on the man, no reason to point out to him that she did not appreciate him playing her. At the same time he needed to know that she was onto him.

"Weren't you with Heddy at Carlos and Charlie's last evening?" she asked.

"I was, and what would be the significance in that?"

"Suppose you tell me?"

"You're jealous," Marc said.

"I am not."

But deep down she knew that she was jealous, and she was having a hard time dealing with her emotions. She needed to get away from him.

"I've got to go," Serena said, racing off.

When she reached her suite, she heard voices, which meant Pia had a visitor.

"Pia, is that you?" Serena inquired.

"Who else would it be?.We have a guest, *querida*."

Out on their veranda, Tracy and Pia were having breakfast. Serena wasn't quite sure how she felt about this new friendship. There was something about Tracy she just didn't trust.

Pia held out a tray of fruit.

"Want some?"

Serena helped herself to a piece of mango.

Tracy looked awfully comfortable on one of the chaise loungers. She wore dark glasses and it was disconcerting not to see her eyes.

"Pia was telling me you lost your purse, and that a guard found it," Tracy said. "You were lucky."

Serena took a seat in the lounger facing the entertainer. "Why lucky?"

"Because ships are like floating cities. People steal things and you never ever see them again. Was anything missing?"

"No. Is that coffee in the carafe?"

Pia got up and poured from the pot, handing Serena a cup.

"You mean you got back money, credit cards and the pendant?" Tracy asked.

"The pendant was in my pocket."

Was it her imagination, or did Tracy flinch? Serena drank her coffee as Pia and Tracy chatted, then she got up and stretched.

"I'm going to take a shower and go back to bed. Nice seeing you again, Tracy."

Later, after a refreshing nap, Serena went to The Rose Petal tearoom for inspiration. She completed the draft of the first chapter of her book and was feeling very pleased about that. Selena would have been happy with what she'd done so far. Serena even had a working title, *A Shepherd's Dream*.

Satisfied with her efforts, she snapped her laptop shut and went in search of Diego, who'd said he would be in the Polaris Lounge for most of the day.

When she arrived there were several people on the dance floor, Diego among them. He spotted her and made his way over.

"Hey, good-looking, how are you doing?" He kissed both of Serena's cheeks, continental-style. "You bring your dancing shoes with you?"

"Right here." Serena tapped the canvas tote she was carrying.

Diego was already on the floor, arms out, slim hips gyrating to a Bee Gees tune. Serena quickly changed her shoes and joined him.

"We do it the Latin way," Diego said, with a rock step followed quickly by a ball change. "A good hustle dancer showcases his lady. Now walk, walk, quick ball change. There you go. Side break, you've got it."

Serena followed him effortlessly. He made the hustle look easy. When the music changed to Donna Summer's "She Works Hard for her Money," Diego was in his element.

For the next half an hour they practiced turns, walks and dips, and at the end of the session Serena felt as if she had truly learned how to do the Latin hustle.

She was thanking Diego for his help when she spotted Sal Morena with Heddy Maxwell draped over him. The two were a perfect pair, she thought. Spotting Serena, Sal managed to quickly extricate himself from his partner's grip and came loping over.

"What a pleasure to see the lovely Serena again," he said. "Time for a dance with me?" He leered in the direction of her cleavage.

"No, I'm afraid not. I have to be somewhere and I'm already late." No way did she want to have that man touching her.

"You will be competing in the semifinals later, I hear. I will be there. We shall dance."

Serena managed to smile and almost fled the room.

By then it was midafternoon and she had about half an hour before her salon appointment. She hadn't had lunch and decided to pick up something fast at the Garden Terrace buffet.

Several people must have had the same idea. The lines sampling the various cuisines were long but moved quickly. Serena helped herself to a salad, salmon and wild rice before taking a seat at one of the tables.

Serena wolfed down her meal quickly. She was still unsure what she wanted to do about Marc and his invitation. One half of her wanted to be with him, and the other half said she was only setting herself up for heartbreak again. There was still the matter of his true identity and that feeling he had something to hide.

The beauty salon was enjoying a brisk business when Serena got there. In the waiting area, a number of people were complaining about the ship needing more operators, and inside, every chair was filled. The air was filled with the smell of frying hair, hairspray, and perfumed gels. After a twenty-minute wait, Serena was ushered into a chair.

"What are you having done today?" the stylist asked.

"Wash, trim and my hair put up. I'm going for an elegant look."

For the next hour, Serena allowed the salon attendant to transform her. She was pleased with the result. The stylist had piled her hair high on her head in a cascade of curls. Now she had enough time to take a leisurely shower and put on her makeup before getting dressed for the Rhythym Dancers party and the Captain's cocktail hour.

When she entered her suite she found Tracy helping Pia with her hair.

"I'm sorry," Pia mouthed.

The dancer held a flat iron in her hand and was trying her best to straighten Pia's short curls. Serena made an effort to greet the woman politely. She meant to talk to Pia later about this developing friendship. Pia seemed to feel sorry for the entertainer.

"You look great," Tracy said, checking out Serena's hair. "The salon did a nice job."

"Thanks."

"Gilles Anderson is looking for you," Pia chimed in, passing Serena a note. "He called a couple of times mentioning something about the two of you having plans to play Ping-Pong or practice your dance steps. Anyway, I think he wants to meet up and go to the cocktail party. Call him."

Serena excused herself and entered the bedroom. She stripped off her clothing, wrapped herself in a robe and picked up the phone.

Marc answered on the second ring.

"Hello."

"It's Serena. Pia tells me you called."

"I thought we were supposed to touch base for Ping-Pong and then go over our dance steps?"

"We talked about it but I don't recall making a definite commitment."

"How about I escort you ladies to the Rhythm Dancers Cocktail party. Afterward we can pop into the captain's party."

"That would be lovely." The words slipped out before she could stop them.

"Maybe we can even manage a quick practice."

"Okay."

"I'll meet the two of you in the lobby in an hour, then."

Serena's caution buttons were on high when she hung up. She had an official date with Marc LeClair, a man she knew was lying to her.

She would make sure to guard her heart.

CHAPTER SEVENTEEN

"WHAT HAVE YOU FOUND OUT about the dancer who was with the d'Andrea woman in Cozumel?" Thanasi asked Sean.

He'd stopped by the security office on his way to the dance group's cocktail party. Afterward he'd have to hotfoot it over to the captain's cocktail party to be part of the reception line.

"Tracy Irvine's her name. She's relatively new to the cruise business. She's a Vegas showgirl."

"Anything else we need to know about her?"

Sean tapped the tip of his pen against his desktop. "I'm not sure if this is relevant, but the dancers think she's having a relationship with one of the newly hired escorts. He's been seen coming and going from her room at all hours."

"Hmmm. I wonder if he's the person she was with when your security guard interrupted their argument."

"Entirely possible. Unfortunately it was dark and my man didn't get a good look at the guy before he ran off."

"Have you talked to Tracy?"

"Not at this point."

"Then I suggest you do. Didn't she say something to your man about losing her purse when she was found? Seems a bit strange that two women who were hanging out all day would both lose purses."

"Good point. I'll bring her in."

"Make it sooner than later. You might want to talk with this newly hired escort, as well. Presumably your men did a background check on him?"

"It's standard procedure."

"Try to determine the nature of the relationship. Something here just doesn't feel right."

"I agree," Sean said, standing. "I'll get on it right away."

"Let me know what you find out." Thanasi checked his watch. "I have to go. Beep me if you need me."

"I'll go one better. I'll send someone to find you."

MARC PACED THE LOBBY, waiting for Serena and Pia to show up. Instead of grabbing the first available suit, shirt, and tie, as he was used to doing, he'd decided to go all out. Formal night called for black tie, and he had attended enough black tie events in his diplomatic postings to own several tuxedos. He felt right at home in his shirt with the winged collar and the traditional black bow tie.

He was really looking forward to seeing Serena. The intensity of their lovemaking had shaken him to the core, and confirmed that his feelings for her were real. It wasn't just about a quick hop in the sack. He cared for her deeply.

Serena stepped off the elevator, garnering the attention of everyone in the surrounding area. She floated toward him in her silver gown. The clinging dress contrasted nicely with her tanned skin. She'd kept her jewelry simple—dangling earrings, a bracelet and the silver pendant around her neck.

She looked especially regal with her dark hair piled in ringlets on top of her head. And in her three-inch silver heels she was taller than he remembered. The tug in Marc's groin told him this was going to be one long, uncomfortable night.

As he crossed the lobby, he could see that Serena's gown was cut daringly low in the back, baring more flawless skin. Erotic memories of their intimate interlude filled his head.

"You're beautiful," he said, his voice hoarse. He glanced around. "Where's your roommate?"

"Thank you. Pia wasn't quite ready. She said she would catch up with us later. You look very handsome, by the way." She giggled, seeming nervous—not something he associated with Serena.

He linked his fingers through hers. "Shall we head for The Marco Polo and our cocktail party?"

"Lead the way."

They got onto the elevator along with several passengers. Outfits ran the gamut, anything from ballroom gowns and tuxedos to sequined jeans and studded jackets.

On Bacchus, all signs pointed to the Asian restaurant. Judging by the noise level, the dance group's cocktail party was underway.

After being persuaded by yet another photographer to pose for pictures, Marc and Serena entered the Marco Polo. They sidestepped waiters wheeling trays of dim sum and others balancing trays, finally finding a spot in the packed room.

Marc shouted over the noise. "This is a zoo. How about I grab some champagne? We'll take our drinks with us to the upper deck and have a quick practice session before attending the captain's cocktail party."

"Sounds good to me."

Marc managed to grab two flutes of champagne from a passing waiter.

"What about food? Shall I brave the crowd and grab us something to munch on?"

Serena shook her head. "No, I'll wait until the captain's cocktail party."

A hand trailed Serena's naked back. The intimate touch and her horrified expression made Marc pay closer attention.

An accented voice said, "*Bella,* you are by far the most beautiful woman here tonight, and your jewelry complements that dress perfectly. You will save me a dance later, yes?"

For just one moment Marc saw the look of disdain in Serena's eyes before she shuttered them. She needed rescuing, and he was just the man for the job.

"Honey, I hate to break this up, but we need to move on to our next engagement," Marc said, placing his arm possessively around Serena's waist and beginning to maneuver her toward the exit.

Sal Morena stood his ground.

"You will save me a dance later," he repeated, his eyes intense. "We dance well together."

"We need to go," Marc said firmly.

Outside, Serena whooshed out a breath.

"What an awful man. He's always showing up out of nowhere and staring at me. He acts like I'm his lunch, and he keeps staring at the pendant. I think maybe this is the last time I'll wear it."

Serena touched the hollow of her neck as if to reassure herself the pendant was still there.

"Why would he be so interested in it?"

She pursed her lips. "He says he's a jeweler, but I'm not sure I believe him."

"I think he's probably just interested in you," Marc said.

"I'm afraid you might be right," Serena agreed.

They climbed the winding stairs up to the open deck. Here the smell of the ocean was more evident. A cool breeze ruffled Serena's curls and she tilted her head back, drinking in the tangy air. A barely discernible moon was making its appearance.

Marc hugged Serena, pressing his forehead against hers. They remained like this for a while, gently swaying. It felt so right holding her. He reveled in the delicious smell of her perfumed body and freshly shampooed hair.

"I thought we were supposed to be practicing our rhythm dancing," she said against his ear.

"I'm waiting for the right music to come on."

She laughed lightly. "There is no music. Shall we make some?"

"I thought you'd never ask." His lips grazed her temple as he brought her firmly against him. He enjoyed this lady so much.

Serena's arms locked around his neck. He cupped the sides of her face and tilted her head back, forcing her to look him in the eye.

"I have a confession," Marc said, "But first I need to do this."

His head dipped and he covered her waiting mouth, drinking deeply of her. Marc showed her with his tongue what he would like to do to her body should she give him the chance.

Something, a second sense maybe, caused him to look up. He shoved Serena away from him and then dove. As he hit the deck, headfirst, he heard the sound of ripping clothes. A millisecond later, a lounge chair came crashing down.

Footsteps thudded toward them. A woman screamed. Voices came at him from everywhere.

"Oh, my God! Someone get a doctor. These people need help."

"Where's the cruise staff?"

"Please, someone call the front desk."

And then there was blackness.

THANASI WAS STANDING in the reception line at the cocktail party when his beeper went off. Talk about poor timing. He shook the hands of the wealthy couple occupying one of the owner's suites, and made a halfhearted promise to visit them on his vacation. It would never happen. He seldom fraternized with guests off ship, and he'd had plenty of opportunity.

After they moved on, he looked down, glancing at his beeper. Someone at the Guest Relations Desk was paging him. It must be important. Thanasi tried to catch Patti's eye but she was being monopolized by one of the male dancers. Thanasi went through the motions, clasping another hand, making the right noises, waiting for the right moment to find out why he was wanted.

His beeper vibrated again. He looked up to see one of Sean's men heading his way. Nick spotted him at the same time and they exchanged looks. Excusing himself, Thanasi stepped out of the reception line.

"Are you looking for me?" he asked the officer.

"Yes, sir. Sean said I was to find you wherever you were. You're to meet him in the infirmary."

"Infirmary? What's going on?" Thanasi kept his voice low in the event there were eavesdroppers.

"Two people were hurt, sir. A man and a woman."

Not again. Things were whirling out of control and he didn't seem to be able to stop them. What the hell was he dealing with?

Falling in step with the man, Thanasi hurried toward the employee elevator. Sean was waiting at the entrance of the clinic, two of his men flanking him.

"What's up?" Thanasi greeted him.

"There's been another situation."

"Should I be sitting down for this?"

Sean motioned for him to walk down the hall where they could talk privately.

"A lounge chair fell from an upper deck and narrowly missed hitting two people."

Thanasi raised a skeptical eyebrow. "The chair just fell?"

"My guess is it had help."

"Were the two people involved anyone I know?"

"Yes, d'Andrea and the Canadian, Gilles Anderson."

"Not again."

"The Anderson man got the worst of it. He may have seen it coming and pushed d'Andrea out of the way. She's got scrapes and bruises, possibly a twisted ankle. He hit his head pretty badly and blacked out. He's got some nasty cuts on his face."

"Are they both being seen by the doctor?"

"Yes. The doctor doesn't think their injuries require calling an air ambulance. It was recommended that Anderson go to the hospital in Grand Cayman since it has up-to-date equipment. We're somewhat limited in terms of the kinds of testing we can do onboard."

Thanasi sighed. "It's just been one thing after another since that woman came on board."

"She's determined not to cut short her vacation. She claims she's not going to let a few cuts and bruises stop her from enjoying her cruise."

"What does Anderson say?"

"He's as adamant as she is about not leaving mid-cruise. He says he'll sign a waiver relieving us of responsibility for his health. He'll go to the hospital in Grand Cayman for an MRI but that's it. He's got cruise insurance."

"I'm surprised neither of them are screaming lawsuit," Thanasi said under his breath.

"That hasn't come up yet."

"It will. Now let's see if the good doctor will allow us to speak to both of them. It would figure this would have to happen on formal night."

"A desk job on land is sounding better and better," Sean muttered under his breath.

"At this point it won't take much to twist my arm."

Taking a calming breath, Thanasi followed Sean into the clinic.

CHAPTER EIGHTEEN

TRACY WAS WASHING the heavy theatrical makeup off her face when she heard a knock on her door.

She still ached all over from her fall, and had barely made it through the evening's two performances. At this late hour, she was in no mood for guests.

The knocking continued.

"Ms. Irvine. It's security. Open up."

Tracy let the water trickle through her fingers. What did security want with her?

"Ms. Irvine, it's extremely important we speak with you."

"I'll be right there."

It was useless pretending she wasn't in. Everyone knew everything there was to know on the ship, and what they didn't know they made up.

She threw more cold water on her face, grabbed a towel and patted herself dry. Snatching her robe off a hook on the bathroom door, she slipped into it.

"Yes," she said, opening up and facing two grim-faced security guards she didn't recognize.

"Ms. Irvine, the Acting Chief of Security wants to see you in his office," the taller one said.

"At this hour?"

"Yes, ma'am."

"Doesn't your boss have better things to do on formal night?" she grumbled. "I'll get dressed and be right with you." She shut the door in their faces.

Breathe, Tracy. Take a deep breath!

She wondered if they'd linked her with Sal. Had he gotten caught and fingered her as an accomplice?

Tracy tried not to hyperventilate. She threw on the first thing she found—black leggings and an oversize T-shirt—and slid her feet into ballet slippers. Scooping her hair off her face, she found a scrunchee and bunched it into a ponytail. Then she found her card key and picked up her hobo bag.

Two men flanked her as they escorted her to the security office. This must be what it felt like to be under arrest and not told what you'd done wrong. She was not about to let Sal take her down. From everything she'd heard, Sean's office was not the place you wanted to be. You were usually summoned here when you were about to be fired.

One of the guards tapped on the closed office door.

"Come in."

The second security guard opened the door and stood aside for Tracy. Taking a deep breath, she entered the room.

Sean looked up from a stack of folders he'd been perusing.

"Ms. Irvine, please have a seat." He gestured to the chair facing him.

"I prefer to stand, thank you," she said.

"As you wish. You lost your purse yesterday. Did you ever find it?"

"What purse?" What was he talking about?

Sean gave her a chilling look.

"Last night when you were found on the topless deck, you said something about falling and losing your purse. Did you find it?"

"Oh, that. Yes. It turned up."

"Who were you with in Cozumel yesterday?"

Since she wasn't sure where this was all leading, she decided to stick as closely to the truth as possible.

"I had the day off and spent it with passengers. That's permitted, right?"

"Yes, you're free to socialize on your own time."

"Then why am I here?"

Sean Brady gave her a long, hard stare. It was difficult to figure out what he was thinking.

"Was Serena d'Andrea one of the passengers you were with?" Sean asked.

"Yes."

"Then you must know Serena also lost her purse."

"No, I didn't know that."

Again Sean's icy gaze pinned her.

"You spent the day together and you didn't know Serena lost her purse. It's an amazing coincidence that you would both lose purses."

"It happens."

"Let's talk about Salvatore Morena."

"What about him?"

"He's been seen coming and going from your cabin." Sean was watching her carefully, as if expecting a reaction.

"He's a contracted employee. I thought that was okay."

"You've been heard arguing loudly?"

"We don't always agree."

"Ms. Irvine. Be straight with me."

Tracy looked into Sean's eyes and hoped her fear didn't show. "I have nothing to hide."

"You were pretty banged up when you were found. Was Sal Morena the man who pushed you and caused you to fall?"

"The deck was wet. I slipped and fell." Better to stick to her story.

Sean pressed his fingertips together and continued to stare.

"I'm not sure I believe you," he said after a while. "But I'll let it go for now. You may go."

"Believe what you want. I'm telling the truth."

Ignoring her roiling stomach, Tracy turned to leave. Please God let her make it back to her cabin before she got sick.

As she closed the door behind her she thought she heard Sean say, "Run a background check on Tracy Irvine. I want to know everything there is to know about that woman."

A background check! They might find out she was once married to Sal, and a number of other sordid details she'd hoped no one would ever know.

"HOW ARE YOU HOLDING UP?" Patti asked, coming up behind Thanasi as he sat hunched over his computer. She kneaded his tense shoulder muscles and he inhaled her subtle peach scent.

"I've been better. Have you heard about the latest incident with the d'Andrea woman and her companion?"

"Yes. It gets worse and worse. She's clearly been targeted."

Patti's fingers worked miracles on the tightness he'd been feeling in his neck and lower back. He made circles with his neck, hoping to get out the kinks.

"Lower," he ordered. "And a little to the right."

Patti's splayed fingers moved lower. "Tell me when."

"A little higher."

"How's that?"

"Perfect." Thanasi sighed. He was enjoying Patti's hands on his flesh and the quiet support she provided.

It was late, very late, and he'd stayed up to work on a report Nick would need to send to headquarters. It documented all the incidents onboard to date, and the efforts made by the employees to ensure the safety and security of passengers.

Writing the incident report was only a precautionary effort. Documentation would be necessary in the event the cruise line was sued. It was better to do it now while the situation was still fresh in his brain.

Thanasi was wired, and even though it was late,

sleeping would require some effort. He'd come back to his office determined to get the report done. Once the ship docked in Grand Cayman there would be very little time to complete it.

Patti brought the massage to an end with a firm squeeze of his shoulders. Thanasi would have liked nothing more than to have her massage him forever. He'd missed a woman's touch and he especially enjoyed hers.

"Should I put on a pot of coffee?" Patti asked.

"Only if you join me."

"Of course."

She found coffee, got water and a filter from the utility area, and flicked the switch on the pot. While they waited for the beverage to perk, Patti perched on the edge of his desk. Her skirt hiked up a bit to reveal two toned shapely legs, legs that certainly got his attention.

They were bronzed, athletic, perfectly proportioned and without panty hose. In the Caribbean heat, few of his female crew wore nylons.

"I'm counting the days before vacation," she said, "I never used to before."

"Me, too, and I never thought I would say that." He yawned. "I imagine Ariana's nervous and excited about getting married in a few days."

"Yes, but she tells me marrying Dante feels right. He'll be boarding in a few hours and they'll get to spend some time together before the ceremony."

"Sometimes I wish I had someone to be crazy about popping on board at the various ports."

It was a rare admission for him. He usually avoided these types of personal conversations with his staff. But he'd come to trust Patti and knew she was discreet. She would never repeat what he said.

Patti nodded empathically. "I know what you mean."

"Ship's life can be lonely, and having a loved one's support would make things so much easier."

When Patti uncrossed her legs and walked over to see if the coffee was done, he had to exert every ounce of self-control not to kiss her.

She was making him crazy.

Thanasi got up from the chair, stretched, and yawned. Patti poured two cups of coffee and brought them back. She set them down on his desk. When she reached for her cup, his hand covered hers.

Patti's eyebrows shot up.

"Thanasi…"

"Yes?" He leaned in closer, so close that all he could smell was peach.

And then they were kissing.

It started off as a brush of the lips, but soon developed into a much more passionate encounter. Patti's arms were around his neck and he grasped her buttocks, pressing her into him, at the same time deepening the kiss.

When Patti's breasts grazed his chest, Thanasi reacted like any red-blooded male would. He brought her up hard against him.

"Is that door locked?" she said breathlessly.

"It's late. No one's about to wander in."

"I'm not taking chances."

With a nudge of her hand, she pushed him away and crossed to the door to lock it. Then unbuttoning her blouse, she slowly came back to him.

He was out of his shirt faster than he thought was possible, and helping her out of her skirt. She was wearing only her bra and high cut thong underwear. And she was even lovelier than he'd imagined. He'd fantasized about her for a long time but this was even better than his fantasies.

He hooked a finger in the front of her bra. The clasp broke, spilling her breasts into his hands. He bent his head, capturing a nipple in his mouth and tugging on it gently. Patti's moan made him lose any pretense of civility. She reached for his zipper.

Sweeping the paperwork off his desk, he hoisted Patti onto the hard surface. Her fingers clawed his back. Thanasi's mouth nipped and sucked the sides of her neck. He'd wanted to do this forever.

Making love to her was beyond sweet. She was beyond sweet. He'd broken his own golden rule: never get involved with one of his employees. Business and pleasure weren't a good mix.

But Patti Kennedy was proving to be the exception.

CHAPTER NINETEEN

SERENA HAD BEEN LOOKING forward to the Grand Cayman shore excursion, but now with a twisted ankle and an aching shoulder, she doubted she'd even be able to swim with the stingrays.

The outcome could have been far worse, she supposed. Thankfully Marc had pushed her out of the way when that lounge chair came tumbling down. Unfortunately he had gotten hurt in the process and was off to the hospital for an MRI. Serena was worried about him.

Balancing most of her weight on the metallic walking stick with the claw feet the doctor had given her, she hobbled from her suite. If she was going to be stuck onboard she might as well smell the sea.

As an afterthought she decided to take her laptop with her. She made sure the pendant was tucked into the case. She was planning to hand it in early, but until she did, she wasn't going to risk losing it.

Serena nodded at the security guard stationed in the hallway before getting on the elevator. She took it one floor to Artemis and slowly made her way toward Sunshine's American Diner. Sitting around the pool in the sun wouldn't be so bad.

After placing her order, she sat, eyes closed, soaking in the sun. She thought about Marc and wondered how things were going at the hospital. He'd fought with the cruise ship personnel not to be sent home. Going to the hospital in Grand Cayman had been a compromise.

Removing her laptop from its case, she turned it on and checked to see if the velvet pouch with the pendant was still tucked into the corner. She'd been wearing the pendant when that lounge chair came crashing down. She was always wearing the pendant when horrible things happened, and she had to assume it wasn't just coincidence.

When her food was served she ate it quickly. She was now at a point in her manuscript where the upper middle class heroine had met her working class hero, and was trying to figure out how to introduce him to her snobbish parents.

Class still mattered in South America, and a young readership would be able to relate to her heroine's dilemma. She chewed on the tip of her pencil, considering how to heighten the internal conflict between hero and heroine.

"How are you doing?" a female voice asked. "Pia told me you had an accident and hurt your ankle."

Tracy was standing above her.

"Managing and trying to forget about the incident."

What was it with Tracy? She kept showing up in the most unexpected places. She and Sal were two of a kind.

The dancer plopped down next to her. "So what actually happened?"

"A chair fell from the deck up above."

"No! You were lucky to just have a twisted ankle." Tracy sounded both surprised and outraged. She eyed Serena's walker. "Did the doctor give you that?"

"Yes."

"It's that pendant again. I bet you'll be glad to see the last of it."

"What do you mean?"

Tracy lowered her voice and leaned in closer. "Can I trust you?"

"My lips are sealed."

"Every time someone finds that pendant there's been problems."

"Really? I thought it was supposed to bring me luck in love?"

"That's what they tell you, but there's been an issue on every single voyage. I could hold it for you for safekeeping until the end of the cruise. Or you could give it to Kali at the front desk and tell her that you no longer want any part of it."

"I'll think about it," Serena said, shutting down the laptop and standing. "I have to go. I scheduled a massage and I'm running late."

"Let me know what you decide," Tracy called after her.

The hell she would. Serena did not trust the woman and had the strangest feeling she was involved in her recent spate of bad luck. But why waste the day? She had no massage scheduled. The swelling had gone down on her ankle and she could put a little more weight on it now. If she took a taxi into Georgetown, the capital, she could fit in some nonstrenuous sightseeing.

She returned to her suite, took the pouch with the pendant from the laptop's case and tucked it into her bra. Then, grabbing her camera and cane, she hobbled off to catch the next tender.

On shore she found a cab quickly, but unfortunately the stores closed early on Saturdays so that ruled out any shopping other than souvenirs.

"Take me to Hell," Serena said impulsively. She'd read about the tourist attraction with the black limestone formation that looked as if it had been burned by hell's flames.

"Not much there, mom," her driver said, "Just a gas station, some shops and the post office. Tourists just love buying postcards so they can send greetings from Hell." He chuckled at his own wit and took off.

Serena thought it might be fun to take photographs of the area. When the driver slowed down, she spotted a large sign announcing they'd arrived in Hell. Just as her cab driver had indicated, there wasn't much other than the formation. Tourists were taking pictures in front of the sign, and a few shops were filled with people buying post cards and T-shirts.

"You want me to wait for you, mom?" the taxi driver asked when Serena took out her purse.

"If you can. How much would it cost?"

After some haggling they agreed on a price.

"You be careful with that foot, hear," he shouted at her as she left. "There are plenty of stones."

Serena purchased a half dozen postcards at one of the shops and hobbled over to the post office. At the entrance was a costumed devil holding a pitchfork.

"Welcome to hell," the devil said, bowing and sweeping his cape in front of him. He pointed to a sign: Satan works for tips.

Several tourists began pleading to take photos with him. He agreed to do so for a nominal fee. Serena wrote a few quick notes, addressed her cards, and waited in line to buy stamps.

Afterward a woman offered to take her picture in front of the post office. Photo taken, Serena carefully made her way toward one of the two viewing platforms where tourists were permitted to stand.

She stood among a crowd of awed tourists looking down at the rock formation, which brought to mind images of brimstone. An eerie and all too familiar feeling came over her. She was certain she was being watched. Goosebumps rose on her arms.

Aiming her camera, she got off several shots. Someone jostled her elbow and she dropped the camera. As she bent to retrieve it, she was pulled back by the strap of her bag. It was ripped from her shoulder, and she would have fallen except for several steadying hands. People were screaming, panicked.

"Thief! Thief!" someone shouted.

"It's the devil himself."

"Catch that man! He stole that woman's purse."

Screna's ankle had started to throb. Someone helped her to her feet and she looked around for the missing cane. Her arm hurt now.

Some local men were chasing the masked man. He looked just like the devil at the post office, hurtling over rocks as if he had some supernatural power. Two of the men were closing in on him, and people were screaming and cheering.

"You almost got him. Go man, go!"

One of the men took a flying leap, landing on the devil's back. He tried to shake off his human cargo but was unsuccessful. The other man converged, tackling him to the ground.

Serena's pounding heart matched the throbbing in her ankle. Someone had to be watching her every move and following her. She needed her purse. It had her money to pay the cab driver. She patted her chest, reassured the pendant was still in her bra.

The devil was being pulled to his feet. He held her purse in his hand. Someone yanked off his mask. People began screaming questions at him. He looked like a native of the island. But why had he chosen her of all people? Maybe it was just that her walking stick had made her a likely target. But she didn't think so.

"There's the constable," the woman next to her shouted. "This kind of thing reflects badly on our island."

"They'll want to talk to you," one of the tourists who'd helped her said.

"Where's my cane?"

Some one handed Serena the missing cane. With help, she was escorted to the area where the thief was being apprehended by a second policeman.

"That's the woman whose purse was stolen," one of the locals pointed out.

The policeman handed her her purse, instructing her to check inside. She quickly looked to make sure her wallet was there and generously tipped the men who'd helped to catch the thief.

"You'll need to come to the precinct with us," one of the policemen said.

Serena paid the taxi driver and was then led to a van. At the precinct she was questioned and filled out several forms. The thief turned out to be the man who was posing as the devil in front of the post office. He told the police that he'd been paid by a tourist to steal Serena's bag, and described the man as "Tall, white, medium build, with dark hair."

Because the devil had a long record of petty thefts, he was handcuffed and taken away to a cell.

By the time Serena left the precinct she was wrung out. She barely made it in time to catch one of the last tenders back to the ship. Her ankle was even more swollen now, and the cruise staff called for a wheelchair to get her to her suite.

As she waited, she realized it was time to give the pendant back.

But not before she found out if it was valuable.

"WHEELCHAIR NEEDED on the lower deck."

The announcement boomed over Patti Kennedy's radio.

"Chief Steward come in," Patti said into her handset. "Wheelchair needed."

Ariana Bennett overheard the transmission even though she was off duty. She still had her radio on. She was sitting in the lobby, watching the predinner cruise crowd come back from shore. She'd rushed off to the airport to get Dante, but his flight had been delayed, and there wasn't an estimated time of arrival yet, so she'd returned to the ship to wait.

Ariana flagged Patti down as she went by. "Can I help?"

Patti sighed loudly. "This is the fourth request for a wheelchair today. I don't know what it is about Grand Cayman that makes people careless. Hopefully we have another chair somewhere. You look nice."

"Thanks." Ariana laughed. "It's cost me my entire salary at the salon to look this good. Want me to check with the chief steward and see if he has some extra chairs tucked away someplace?"

"If you wouldn't mind, but aren't you off duty? I thought your man was coming in?"

"Dante's flight is delayed. The airline personnel don't seem to know exactly when he'll be here."

Patti's beeper went off. She glanced at it, read the text message and groaned.

"The chief purser says it's that South American woman who's been hurt. She's a VIP and he can't hand her off to just anyone."

"Why don't I find a wheelchair and take it down to her. I'm good at schmoozing. Besides, I like Serena d'Andrea."

"But you're on your day off."

"That means I have more time on my hands than you. As I said, I like Serena and I don't mind. She's been coming into the library almost every day and she's always been gracious."

"Okay, if you're sure." Patti's beeper went off again. This time she looked down and turned scarlet. "Everyone wants a piece of me today. Now it's our illustrious hotel director."

"I think he wants more than a piece of you." Ariana winked, then hurried off to find the chief steward.

She managed to persuade him to find a chair, but he insisted on wheeling it down to the lower deck himself, where they were able to seat Serena. The steward got beeped again and quickly headed off to another call.

"You must have done quite a bit of walking on that foot," Ariana said, as she pushed Serena in the direction of her penthouse suite.

"I did do some walking before I found a taxi to take me to Hell. Some crook tried to steal my bag and in the process I slipped and fell."

"I hope you reported it to the police. Grand Cayman used to be one of our safest destinations, but like everything else, things change."

"The man was caught but I had to go to the precinct and fill out paperwork." Serena sighed loudly.

Ariana placed a reassuring hand on her shoulder and squeezed.

"Things will get better. You have a day and a half

at sea to rest up before we head for some of our more popular ports. You've got St. Thomas, St. Maarten, Dominica, St. Vincent and Barbados all coming up. They're beautiful islands."

At the penthouse Serena got out her card key.

The door opened before they could unlock it.

"I was worried about you," Serena's elegant roommate said. "What's with the wheelchair?"

Serena pointed to her leg. "It's not as bad as it looks. My ankle's swollen and a little sore. It should be okay in a day or so as long as I stay off it." She fumbled thorough her purse looking for a tip.

"Absolutely not," Ariana said, stopping her. "It's been my pleasure. I'll look forward to seeing you in the library soon. The butler will be up shortly with ice for that ankle."

"Thank you."

Nodding to both women, she left, hoping this was the last mishap on the cruise.

CHAPTER TWENTY

"MAY I SPEAK WITH SERENA, please?" Marc asked when a female voice answered the phone. He assumed it was her roommate, Pia, who'd answered. It was his third call and the first time the phone had actually been picked up.

"Who's calling?" the woman asked.

"Marc—uh—Gilles," Marc stammered.

"Which one is it? Marc or Gilles?"

He cleared his throat. Serena's roommate sounded as if she was onto him.

"It's Gilles Anderson."

"Ah, Gilles. Serena may already be asleep. If she's awake I'll let her tell you about her trip to Grand Cayman."

"Grand Cayman? I thought she was resting up."

Through the earpiece Marc heard muffled voices, then Serena came on the phone.

"How did it go at the hospital?" she asked, sounding amazingly low key and not like the bubbly woman he knew.

"Long, tedious, with lots of questions and paperwork. I don't think the nurses were familiar with cruise insurance."

"And your tests?" she probed.

"They came back fine. I had a mild concussion. The doctor signed off, and here I am. What about you? What's this I hear about you going into Grand Cayman? I thought you were supposed to be resting."

"I got bored."

He chuckled. That sounded just like Serena. "Why don't you join me for a drink before dinner and tell me all about your jaunt."

Serena's hesitation came through loud and clear. He held the receiver, waiting.

At last she said, "I'm not very mobile."

"What does that mean?"

"Um, I hurt my ankle again."

"I'll be right down," Marc said, hanging up before she could say another word.

A COUPLE OF HOURS LATER, Sadie Bennett's voice came through the static of the ship to shore call, grounding Ariana in reality.

"Honey, it's just a few days before your wedding. You must be getting nervous. Is there anything you need?"

"No. It's all been taken care of. I only have my dress left to get and I'll buy it in St. Maarten."

Ariana should never have picked up the phone. She and Dante had just made love and they were still in that euphoric state where the only thing that mattered was the two of them. Dante had arrived just minutes before sailing and they had quickly made up for lost time.

"Get something nice," Sadie insisted. "If you

don't have time, I might be able to find a dressmaker here to whip you up something quickly."

"I have it under control, Mom," Ariana repeated. "Patti and I are going shopping together."

But Sadie refused to leave it alone.

"I know the shipboard ceremony is supposed to be casual, but you still need to look presentable."

Ariana smothered a groan. Dante brought her close, kissing her temple. She inhaled his musky male smell and burrowed farther under the covers.

"I will, Mother. I promise."

The conversation was getting old. She'd told Sadie time and time again she was a big girl and could quite efficiently handle her own wedding details. But her mother seemed more concerned than she. You would think she was the one getting married.

"Please don't penny pinch," Sadie continued, refusing to drop the subject. "Get something beautiful. I'll reimburse you whatever the cost. It is your special day."

This time Ariana did groan out loud.

"Indulge me. I am your mother." Sadie chuckled. "What's going on onboard anyway? Nick and Elias are constantly on the phone. I keep overhearing talk about a publishing heiress being attacked—the woman who found the pendant."

"There've been several issues involving the passenger but we're not sure what's the cause. She's quite wealthy and someone could be looking to kidnap her."

"You know, it might just have something to do with the pendant. You told me you and Patti based the treasure hunt on the legend of the moon goddess. These teardrop pendants were often used to conceal an offering to one of the goddesses. Maybe somebody thinks there's something hidden inside, especially after the smuggling on the Mediterranean cruises."

"You could have a point, Mom," Ariana mused, then glanced over at Dante. Right now she had other things to think about.

"I'll see you in a few days at the wedding. Love you."

"Love you, baby. Call me if you need anything."

"I will."

Ariana hung up the phone and rolled onto her back.

"Mama still planning our wedding for us?" Dante asked, his deep, husky voice warming her.

"Something like that."

She closed her eyes, snuggling closer to the man she loved with her heart and soul. Dante placed a possessive arm around her and brought her up against him. And although she was an enthusiastic and willing partner in their lovemaking, she just couldn't shake the feeling Sadie might be onto something.

She had to get her hands on that pendant.

NOT BEING ENTIRELY AMBULATORY was putting a crimp in Serena's style. She hated using a cane. The only good thing was that she was forced to work on her book and she'd actually made progress. The story was really taking shape and Selena would have loved the plot.

Marc had become overly attentive when he found out what had happened on Grand Cayman. He'd taken to escorting her around the ship. They'd run into Heddy a time or two and the woman had acted as if Serena had stolen her most valued possession.

Serena felt a little guilty that Marc was missing out on the cruise events. She'd urged him to find another dance partner, but he would hear nothing of it. They no longer stood a chance of winning the dance competition, and she felt responsible for that.

Marc had even decided not to get off in St. Thomas because Serena had opted to stay aboard and rest her ankle. She had made a conscious decision to save herself for the southern Caribbean and islands like Dominica, St. Vincent, Barbados, and St. Lucia, which everyone said she just had to see.

When it rained nonstop for the next couple of days, she convinced herself that she wasn't missing much. She'd overheard passengers who'd purchased tickets for the water sports complaining bitterly about cancellations.

During those dismal days, Serena spent more and more time in the library. She did take a break to get off in St. Maarten but stayed on the Dutch side close to the ship. Much as she'd wanted to see Dominica today, she couldn't risk hurting her ankle again. The island known for its many rivers had experienced floods and mudslides.

So she'd stayed put writing, and already she was a quarter of the way through her book and feeling very good about it.

Her nights were spent with Marc, and each time they made love she felt closer to him. She had encouraged him to see Dominica while she remained onboard writing.

But she just didn't feel her usually optimistic self today. In a few days the cruise would end and she and Marc would go their separate ways. She had a career and family in Buenos Aires and couldn't see herself chucking everything and moving to Alberta or Texas with him. Not that he'd asked her.

Serena was beginning to think their romance was as ill-fated as the moon goddess's. Maybe she needed to put an end to it now and move on.

"Everything okay?" Ariana asked, probably noticing her glum face.

"I was just thinking that in a few days the cruise will end and Ma—Gilles and I will be going our separate ways. I'll miss him."

"I miss Dante, my fiancé, the second he's away from me," Ariana confessed. "We're getting married in a few days and I'm moving to Italy. I can't wait. I hope you will come to both the wedding and reception."

"I plan on it."

Serena had been introduced to Dante Colangelo; the man had the stunning good looks of a movie star.

Ariana had told her all about the ceremony they'd planned aboard ship when they arrived in Barbados.

Since there was no one else in the library, Ariana took the chair opposite Serena's. She leaned over and gave her a hug.

"I just want everyone to be as happy as I am. This has been one heck of a cruise for you. After all you've been through, you deserve to find true love."

"I'd like nothing more, although at times I regret finding that stupid pendant."

"Bring the pendant with you the next time you come to the library?" Ariana suggested. "I've almost forgotten what it looks like. Where's your man today, anyway?"

"Off exploring Dominica in the rain."

"What a guy. Nothing stops him."

The two women continued chatting and discovered they had several things in common, above all a love of books. When Ariana said she was also working on a book, Serena gave her a business card and invited her to submit her completed manuscript to her family's publishing house.

"I'm guessing you're a very good writer," Serena said.

"I think so, but I'll let you be the judge of it."

Rain pelted the window panes and the sky had turned an ominous black by the time Serena left the library. Pia, who'd ventured out earlier, returned to the ship soaked. She'd gone up to the spa for a massage and a seaweed wrap.

Curiosity brought Serena to the Polaris Lounge to

watch the International Standard finals. She took a seat at the back of the room as the dancers in their elaborate costumes circled the floor. Heddy, who'd found herself another partner, had made the finals.

"Ah, *bella,* I have missed you," a voice said close to Serena's ear. She inhaled the stifling smell of a cloying cologne and tried not to gag.

"Hi Sal," Serena said pleasantly, "Don't they ever give you a day off? I thought for sure you would be ashore."

"Not in this weather. I thought you might be staying on board and it would be the perfect opportunity to become better acquainted. I see so little of you now that you are not dancing." His finger caressed the hollow of Serena's throat. "You aren't wearing the pendant today?"

Serena went still inside. She tried not to show her revulsion.

"No. It's a little heavy."

"A shame, because it looks wonderful on you."

"Excuse me, I do have to go," Serena said, standing. She knew she was being rude, but Sal repulsed her.

"Where is your boyfriend today?" he called after her.

"Boyfriend?" She turned back, eyeing him warily.

"The Canadian? I do not think he is man enough for you. You need a real man like me."

"I really do have to go," she said, bolting from the room. What an awful man!

Serena returned to her suite to find a note from

Pia, who was now meeting Andreas for a drink. Since she wasn't sure when she would be back, she suggested Serena make her own dinner plans.

Spotting an envelope on the floor, Serena bent to retrieve it. Her name was written on the front.

She read the note and folded it back into its envelope. Marc had asked her to meet him on Helios later. He said he would have a surprise waiting for her. The odd thing was that he'd asked her to wear the pendant. What was it with men and this pendant?

She decided to think positively. Maybe the tear shaped pendant was going to bring her luck in love after all.

With several hours left until the appointed meeting time, Serena flipped through the ship's daily newsletter. Her choices were a napkin folding lesson, a wine-tasting event, or a game show. She decided to take a nap instead.

Hours later, feeling much more refreshed, she entered the Rose Petal tearoom. It was still raining and more and more people were back on board. They sat sipping tea and commiserating about the miserable weather conditions.

Cup of tea in hand, Serena stood in front of the portrait of Alexandra Rhys-Williams Stamos. There was something about the woman's style and calm dignity she found soothing.

"Lovely, isn't she?"

Serena turned to see Patti Kennedy behind her. The cruise director was wearing her dress whites as it was another formal night.

"She's beautiful. This portrait has fascinated me from the first day I laid eyes on it."

"It fascinates a lot of people and is a very valuable piece. Elias had the diamond pendant specially commissioned for Alexandra. It's a copy of an original."

"How romantic. He must have adored her."

"She was his everything." Patti's beeper went off. "I have to go. Will you be around later?"

"Yes, I'll probably be on the promenade."

"I'll see you there."

After Patti rushed off, Serena stood for a very long time staring at the portrait. She wanted the kind of love that Elias Stamos had with Alexandra. Could she even hope to have that with Marc?

Was it her imagination or did Alexandra Rhys-Williams Stamos's mouth curve into a wide smile, and one lid lower in a conspiratorial wink?

Serena was feeling much more optimistic when she returned to her suite to get ready. As she slipped into her red cocktail pantsuit, she decided to live in the moment and fully enjoy whatever time she had left with Marc. He'd asked her to wear the pendant, and so she would. After rummaging around in the usual hiding places and not finding it, she realized that she'd left it in the pocket of his bathrobe the night before.

On the off chance Marc might be back on board, she went to his cabin first, but he did not respond to her knock. Dinner was about to start in a few minutes and she would check back after she had eaten.

Serena was anxious to talk to Marc about her conversation with Patti. She'd hoped that they could look at the pendant together.

When dinner was over, Serena declined the invitation from her table mates to attend the late show. She returned to Marc's cabin and knocked again. No answer. Could he have come and gone?

She made a quick stop at her suite to freshen up, scribbled a note for Pia telling her she was meeting Marc on Helios, and headed off.

The late show was still in progress as she wandered through the ship. Those having dined early were either at the casino or talking quietly on the promenade. The rain had eased a bit but she couldn't help wondering why Marc had chosen such an isolated spot to meet up.

The Observation Deck was poorly lit and Serena had second thoughts about venturing out onto the wet, slick surface.

Was she being foolish pursuing this relationship? But she couldn't imagine Marc not being in her life. At the same time, she had a career that she enjoyed, and parents who expected her to take over their publishing house eventually. She couldn't just walk away from that responsibility. She was the only child they had left, and they still hadn't gotten over the heartbreaking hurt of losing her twin.

A tear slid down Serena's cheek and she brushed it away.

Fingers trailed her back. Marc was here. He'd made it. Her mood shifted from dismal to joyous.

"Marc, darling. I was so worr…"

"Ah, so it is he who is making you cry," Sal Morena said, standing so close to her she was forced to step back. "Do not waste your tears on someone so unworthy. Not when I am here."

Serena swallowed the lump that had settled at the back of her throat. "I'm okay, really I am, or at least I will be in a few minutes."

"I will wait. You cannot be left alone."

"No, no, it's really not necessary. I just needed some fresh air."

"You will do as I say," he said in an amazing turn about, clamping a large paw around her upper arm and tugging her toward the exit. A gold ring on his middle finger glimmered in the artificial light.

"Stop it! Take your hands off me!" She opened her mouth to scream.

"Shut up! Be quiet! I am now in charge."

Something long, shiny, and cold pressed against her throat. Serena whimpered.

"Where's the pendant? Why are you not wearing it as you were asked?"

How did Sal know that Marc had asked her to wear the pendant tonight? The answer was like a cold glass of water tossed in her face. Marc wasn't the one who'd written the note.

Sal gave her arm another tug. "I am talking to you. You will answer me. I want that pendant. It is mine in payment for a gambling debt."

Rain splattered down on Serena's head, drops forming on her eyelashes, and trickling down her cheeks. They mingled with the salt of her tears. Sal whistled and in the darkness another whistle replied, like a mating call.

Coming down the staircase was Tracy Irvine. In her hands she carried a thick coil of rope.

Tracy. Serena had sensed there was something off about the woman. The two were in this together.

"She does not have the pendant, or at least says she does not," Sal barked when Tracy was closer. "You will need to do a full body search."

Over Serena's dead body. "Don't you dare!"

Sal's raucous laughter repelled her.

"You are in no position to call the shots, little heiress. We shall see just how much money your family is willing to dish out to get you back. You may be worth far more than any diamond."

Diamond? What was he talking about? Serena remembered Patti Kennedy's earlier conversation in the tea room. Elias had given his bride a beautiful diamond necklace. But what did it have to do with the pendant? Could there be a diamond inside the teardrop pendant?

If Sal and Tracy wanted that pendant so badly, she'd be safe until they found it. She could pretend to cooperate.

CHAPTER TWENTY-ONE

SERENA'S TEETH CHATTERED as she was dragged across the open deck. A cold, wet rain stung her face and drenched her clothing. Tracy had a hold on one arm and Sal the other. They led her toward an area that was even darker and more secluded. She could feel the cold blade of the knife against her neck and her ankle throbbing mercilessly.

She was pressed against the railing. Her first thought was they might toss her overboard just as they'd done to the cabin steward.

Think, Serena. Come up with a plan.

A phone clipped to Sal's waistband jingled.

"I have the woman," he grunted. "I will bring her down the stairs but it will be a slow process in the dark…yes I know we do not have much time…yes, I know the ship is set to sail soon."

"Where are you taking me?" Serena asked when Sal twisted her arm behind her back.

"Some place where no one will find you unless your family comes through with money." His ugly laughter rang out and goose bumps popped out on her arms. "Tracy will check you over to make sure you haven't stashed the diamond in some intimate place."

Gross! What a pig he was.

"Searching me would be useless and a waste of time," she said. "I don't have it with me."

"Then where is it?"

"I left it in a cabin."

"Liar! We have searched your suite. We broke in to the safe. There is nothing there."

"It's not in my suite. I gave it to a friend for safe-keeping."

"You had better not be playing games," Sal threatened, trailing the sharp edge of the knife against her neck. Serena swore she felt blood trickling down her skin, or was it rain?

She was taking a big gamble, hoping and praying that if she led them to Marc's stateroom, he would be there, or maybe someone would see them.

"Let's go," Sal bellowed, shoving her in the direction of a stairway.

Tracy hadn't uttered a word so far. She simply did whatever Sal said. What kind of hold did he have on her?

MARC OPENED HIS EYES to a thudding headache and blackness wherever he looked. He scrambled to understand what had happened as he tried to sit up. His movements were restricted. He was in an uncomfortable position with his arms confined behind him. He couldn't even move his wrists.

His last lucid memory was of returning to the ship

drenched and checking his e-mails before heading to his room and ordering a pot of coffee from room service. He'd been relieved to find an e-mail from his boss with good news. It was over. Santos Guerrera, the drug lord, the man responsible for threatening his life and forcing him out of Colombia, had been caught. Marc was free to end the charade and pursue Serena.

And that was all he could think about. Coming clean. He would talk to Serena and make her understand why he had done what he had. He couldn't have risked her life by getting her involved in his mess. She had to understand that any deception on his part was simply to protect her.

A knock on Marc's door had distracted him. Hoping it was Serena, or at least the coffee, he'd gone to answer it. That was the last thing he remembered.

The knock had been much like the one he heard now, a rapid staccato. Only this time he couldn't answer it because he couldn't move. His head felt as if someone had taken a hammer to it. The ringing phone didn't help.

Pick up the phone, Marc. Call for assistance. Get a doctor.

Marc's brain knew what he should do, but his screaming limbs couldn't cooperate. The knock had now turned into a banging and the ringing phone made his head thud even more.

He tried to roll over, tried to move in the direction of the door. He tried kicking out, even screaming. But his tongue was heavy and his scream became a groan.

The phone stopped ringing then started right up again. Slowly the fog in his head started to clear. He was lying on his back, on the floor in his cabin. There were people at his door. He could hear them calling his name.

"Mr. Anderson, are you inside?"

Anderson? Who the heck was that? Right. That's what his paperwork said. He'd been traveling under an assumed identity. His passport and ticket provided by the Canadian government said he was Gilles Anderson. Onboard he was a regular Joe and not a high ranking diplomat.

Marc groaned and, summoning all of his energy, managed to roll over.

Keep rolling. Keep rolling! Get to that door.

By sheer willpower he got close to the door but not close enough. The banging hadn't stopped and the phone kept ringing at intervals. Marc's mouth felt as if someone had stuffed cotton in it. His tongue was weighted down.

"Like it or not, we're coming in," a man shouted.

The double bolt slid aside and the lock clicked.

A woman screamed.

"*Dios mío!* Oh, my God. I knew something was wrong."

People were bending over him. A man was at his back doing something to his wrist and ankles. Suddenly he could move his limbs again, slowly, lethargically. He tried to stand but his knees buckled.

Someone helped him into a seated position. That sudden motion made him dizzy and the walls moved back and forth. He had a sour taste in his mouth. An ice bucket appeared under his nose and without apology he used it.

A man was speaking into the phone.

"Yes, he's in the room. It looks like he's been drugged and tied up. What?…Serena d'Andrea?… Now?"

The call ended and the security officer who seemed to be in charge stood before him.

"What's happening with Serena?" Marc asked, although his tongue still felt heavy.

The security officer snapped off the light. "Not now. My man's monitoring the activity in the hallway. They'll be here any minute. Quiet, everyone. We need to let this thing play out."

There was another knock on the door, followed by a familiar voice, a voice that Marc loved and fantasized about.

"Gilles?" Serena called. "Please open up."

The security officer placed a finger to his lips before tiptoeing across the room. He put an eye to the peephole. The three people who'd accompanied him went deadly still. Marc recognized his cabin steward, the hotel director and Serena's roommate, Pia.

The officer made another hand movement, motioning them into the bathroom. Slowly, carefully, and with some assistance, Marc was helped in, too. He sank onto the cool tile floor while the others remained standing. Soon his eyes adjusted to the darkness. In the other room the security man was pressed against the wall.

The lock jiggled and someone entered, closing the door once again. A male voice rasped, "You have exactly five minutes to find that pendant and give it to me. Five minutes, you understand? Now move it."

He shoved his human cargo so hard it hit the wall with a loud thud.

That better not be Serena or Marc would kill the SOB.

"Sal! Don't hurt her. Isn't it enough she's brought you to the pendant?" It was a female voice this time.

"Shut up, bitch." The slap resonated through the room. A woman cried out and then began sobbing.

The door to the stateroom burst open and the light snapped on.

"Police! Get your hands up!"

"Don't move or they'll shoot," the head of security ordered, as a policeman trained his pistol on Sal.

Serena lay in a crumpled heap against the wall where Sal had shoved her. Adrenaline surged through Marc and blood roared in his ears. He turned into a raging bull, charging the man with all the strength he could muster. Swinging his fist, he connected with Sal Morena's nose. Blood trickled.

"Cowardly bastard!"

Marc was about to take another swing when someone grabbed his arm, holding him back.

"Take it easy. Let the police do their jobs." It was the security officer.

Two grim-faced cops took over, handcuffing Sal Morena and his accomplice, the dancer.

The brunette was in tears. She kept saying over and over, "Please, you don't understand. I was over a barrel. He kidnapped my child. He said if I didn't get him the pendant with the diamond, I would never see my son again."

"You'll need an attorney. I'd recommend you contact the American Embassy." Thanasi Kaldis sounded as if he actually felt sorry for her. He turned his back and shook his head. "Get these two out of my sight. You can use our security office to question them."

The police hustled Tracy and Sal out.

Marc raced toward Serena and wrapped her in his arms.

"Tell me he didn't hurt you, honey."

"No. I'm okay. When I figured out you weren't the one who sent me the note, I hoped you'd be in your cabin and I knew they would bring me here. They wanted that pendant."

"What note? I didn't leave you a note."

Serena explained about the message that had been shoved under the door.

"And that's when I became suspicious," Pia interjected, speaking for the first time. "Usually if either of us is staying out for any length of time, we touch base with each other. When I heard nothing more from you, I went up to the deck myself, and that's when I saw Tracy and that thug holding a knife to your throat."

Marc's arms remained tightly wrapped around Serena.

"Pia, it's a good thing you did. I will always be grateful to you." To Serena he said, "Honey, we've had dinner every night for the last few nights. Why would I dump you on formal night then ask you to meet me later?"

"I assumed you were having a good time on the island and didn't plan on being back until late."

"I hate to break this up," the security man interrupted. "The police and authorities are going to need to ask you some questions. Ms. d'Andrea, we'll need you to get the pendant. You'll both have to be looked at by a doctor."

"The pendant is in the pocket of your bathrobe," Serena whispered in Marc's ear. "Can you get it?"

Of course he would. He wouldn't have the woman he loved embarrassed. No one needed to know they were sleeping together.

"You'll have to excuse me," Marc said, heading for the bathroom. He returned minutes later, the velvet pouch in hand, and turned it over to Serena.

"I'm ready," he said to Thanasi Kaldis, who stood waiting. Looping an arm around Serena's shoulders, Marc followed the hotel director from the room. Pia was right behind them.

The lobby buzzed with activity as they made their way toward the hotel director's office. The news of the abduction was already out. Either that, or someone had seen the police come aboard. Every step they took, passengers stopped to question the hotel director.

"What kind of cruise line is this?" Marc overheard someone say.

"Is it true they tried to kill that poor woman?"

"They were going to push her overboard, just like they did to that poor steward."

"Headquarters will get back to you with an official announcement," Thanasi said, hurrying by.

Patti Kennedy waited in front of the hotel director's closed office door. Next to her was Ariana Bennett, the librarian, and a man handsome enough to be the lead in a movie.

They all filed into the room. When the door was closed and locked, Marc faced two men he presumed were detectives. The ship's security guards, who were already inside, hugged the walls.

"Have a seat," one of the detectives said. He waved Marc and Serena toward two empty chairs.

Marc pulled out the chair for Serena but chose to stand. In a protective gesture, he placed his hands on the back of her chair.

"Mr. Anderson, won't you sit?" one of the detectives said. "This may take some time."

Marc had to tell them who he really was. He reached for his wallet, removed his identification, and handed it to the detective nearest to him.

"My real name is Marc LeClair," he said. "I'm a Canadian diplomat. It's a long and involved story why I'm traveling under a fake identity. There were threats made on my life and my government felt it best that I leave Colombia."

Serena's head swiveled. She shot him a look that he wasn't sure how to interpret. He would need to talk to her when they had a private moment and explain.

"Would this situation have anything to do with what's been happening on board?" the other detective asked, giving him a hard look.

"I don't know. But you are welcome to contact the Canadian Embassy to verify what I am saying."

"We will."

The next question was directed to Serena.

"May we see the pendant?"

"Of course." Serena handed over the velvet pouch. "What makes this pendant so special? Is there something we should know?"

"After speaking with the suspects, maybe we'll be able to answer your questions. Meanwhile we'll examine the piece and try to determine its value."

"Perhaps I can help," Ariana Bennett said, stepping forward.

"How so?" the detective asked.

"I'm somewhat of a Greek mythology buff. Pendants like this can be used to conceal offerings to the gods. They've long been used as a gift for brides."

The detective nodded and took the teardrop-shaped pendant from its pouch. He squinted at it. "Looks like a hard silver nugget to me."

"If I may interject…" Ariana's fiancé said. "I'm

Dante Colangelo." Reaching into his pocket, he removed a business card and handed it to the policeman. "I used to be an undercover police officer. A couple of employees were arrested when we uncovered an illegal antiquities ring using this ship for smuggling stolen goods. Several priceless artifacts were confiscated. You can verify what I'm saying with Interpol and the FBI."

The detective glanced at Dante's card before shoving it into his pocket. He examined the pendant carefully.

"If that's the case, I can't imagine anything of value would be left behind."

"Everyone thought it was an inexpensive piece," Patti Kennedy added. "There were reproductions among the authentic antiquities. This pendant was tarnished and didn't look like much. Since the FBI left it behind, we decided to use it for a shipboard activity."

"When the ship repositioned to the Caribbean," Ariana interjected, "we decided to have a treasure hunt with the pendant—guaranteeing love and luck to whoever found it."

The scribbling detective turned to his colleague. "Can you find out what's going on with the perpetrators? We'll need to have this piece looked at."

"I don't recall seeing a visible clasp," Ariana offered, "though there is a soldering seam."

The detective ran a thumb around the edges of the pendant.

"Hmm. You might be onto something. Does your infirmary have an X-ray machine?"

"It does," Thanasi responded.

"Good. Then we should have our answer soon."

Thanasi's hand was already on the door knob. "Let's get Mr. LeClair and Ms. d'Andrea to the infirmary, and then we'll take care of this other piece of business."

Marc stood. "Coming, Serena?" He held out his hand.

Serena hesitated for a moment before taking his hand.

"You bet I am."

CHAPTER TWENTY-TWO

HOURS LATER after being thoroughly checked over by the doctor and grilled by the police, an exhausted Marc sat across from Serena on the promenade.

"It's time we talked," he said.

"I'm open to listening to whatever you have to tell me."

She wasn't about to make it easy for him. There was still that matter of him walking out on her six months ago without explanation or a follow-up call.

He brought her palm to his lips.

"I am sorry for the pain I caused. There was a vindictive drug lord out to get me. I didn't want you involved. There was no way I would endanger your life."

"What about you leaving me in a hotel room sleeping. How do you explain that?"

"You didn't get my note?"

"What note?"

"I left one on the nightstand. It had my phone numbers and e-mail addresses on it."

"I never found it," Serena said. "But when you didn't hear from me what stopped you from calling?" Her eyes didn't leave his face.

Marc thought about that. It had been a tough decision, but he'd believed it was for the best.

"When you didn't initiate contact," he said, "I figured it was better to let you go. And when I found out about the contract on my life, it became a matter of your safety."

"I wish it had been easier to let you go," Serena said wistfully. "I was in love with you."

Marc's fingers curled around hers. "I loved you, too, with all my heart. That's why I did what I did. I'm a diplomat. My profession's not usually dangerous, but my life was threatened by a drug lord because I refused to expedite his mistress's immigration papers."

All the emotions Serena had been holding back threatened to bubble to the surface. So much time had been wasted. She'd been depressed for months and had felt empty and betrayed. What had happened to that note?

"Take me to your cabin," she said, coming to a decision. "Make love to me."

Marc brought her to his feet with him. "Exhausted as I am, I would like nothing better."

Inside they quickly got naked. He guided her to the bed and placed an arm around her neck, resting his forehead against hers.

Things heated up quickly after that, and when they were both close to exploding, he eased into her.

"I've missed you," he said, punctuating his words with each slow thrust.

"I've missed you too," she answered, pulling him close until he felt like an extension of her.

They lay like this, enjoying the feel of each other, then Marc gave her a soul-shattering kiss and she began to shudder.

He thrust deeper, and the first explosion pounded through her body, making her gasp.

Marc was right there with her.

"Serena," he said, "I love you."

The next thing she remembered was sunlight streaming through the picture window. It bathed Marc's cabin in a golden light. He was still out, dead to the world.

Careful not to wake him up, Serena slipped out from under his arm. She stood in the middle of the room naked, hugging herself.

While Marc slept, Serena reflected on the past twenty-four hours and the nightmare they'd been through. Hours had been spent filling out paperwork. Once the pendant had been x-rayed and the diamond discovered, there had been even more questions.

But at least it was over now, and Sal Morena had been arrested. Sal had not admitted to drugging the security guards or pushing the steward overboard, but he did say the diamond in the pendant was to be payment for a gambling debt that Giorgio, the previous first officer, had reneged on.

Tracy Irvine, the dancer, had had a brief involvement with the thug and married him. They'd had a child together. Sal had kidnapped that child and forced Tracy to be his informant. He'd been verbally and physically abusive when she hadn't been able to retrieve the pendant. Tracy and her attorney were now trying to work out a plea bargain so that she did not spend the better part of her son's childhood in jail.

With only a few days of cruising left, Serena should enjoy what little time she and Marc had left. She'd heard wonderful things about St. Vincent and the Grenadines, and she'd read about the Botanical Gardens there, the oldest in the Western Hemisphere. She was looking forward to taking a walking tour with Marc and seeing highlights like the breadfruit tree brought to the island by Captain Bligh.

They'd even talked about hiring a car with a driver and going to the windward part of the island. Marc wanted to climb La Soufriere, the dormant volcano, and Serena planned on taking pictures of the lush valley below.

That evening she and Marc were invited to a pre-wedding dinner party given by Captain Nick Pappas and his fiancée, Helena, for Ariana and Dante. The party was to be held in the captain's private quarters.

Both the hotel and cruise directors would be there, and Serena was curious to see if there was a budding romance on the horizon. Andreas and Pia had also been invited, and so had Sean Brady, the Acting Chief of Security.

It would be a night of toasts and laughter.

And it was. The handpicked group got along well and Ariana reiterated her invitation to Serena and Marc to attend her private reception. When Ariana said out loud that she needed something borrowed to wear to her wedding, Serena offered to lend her the pendant, which had been returned to her after the diamond was removed and the piece photographed.

"Awesome!" Ariana said, kissing her cheek. "I hope you'll both be there tomorrow."

The port of Bridgetown, Barbados, was already visible on the horizon by the time the party ended. Serena and Marc left hand in hand. Her next memory was of Marc whispering in her ear.

"Honey, time to get up. We don't want to be late for Dante and Ariana's wedding."

She moaned, settling more comfortably under the sheets.

"Time to get up, baby."

One eye popped open and then the other.

"You aren't dressed," Serena grumbled.

"You need more time than I do," Marc reminded her, gently poking her in the arm. "I'll pick you up at your suite in an hour."

"Okay, okay, I'm on my way." Serena planted a leg firmly on the ground and shook the fog from her head. The two glasses of champagne she'd had the evening before didn't help. "Where are my clothes?"

Marc handed over her dress and underwear.

"One hour, Serena," he reminded her before she slipped out the door.

An hour later, Marc and Serena joined several passengers in the Starlight Theater to witness the beautiful outdoor ceremony officiated by Captain Pappas and a nondenominational Barbadian minister.

A calypso band played the wedding march as Ariana came slowly down the aisle. She was breathtaking in a strapless, tea length dress that billowed around her ankles. The silver pendant Serena had lent her hung around her neck. A ring of fragrant frangipani circled her head, matching the bouquet she carried.

On one side of her was her mother, Sadie, and on the other, Thanasi, the hotel director, to give her away.

Following Ariana was Patti Kennedy, her maid of honor, dressed in an ocean mist bustier and a wrap skirt that ebbed and flowed as she walked. Judging by the smoldering looks the maid of honor was giving the hotel director, it would be only a matter of time before wedding bells rang for those two.

The groom looked handsomely smart in a dark suit and pristine white shirt. His striped tie matched that of his best man. He smiled at his bride as she came down the aisle and winked at her. A blushing Ariana blew him a kiss.

Serena, caught up in the emotions of the moment, squeezed Marc's hand. He squeezed hers back.

Dante's best man, his old mentor, Colonel Bernardo Morretti, looked awfully proud. He was a tall, lanky, middle-aged man with a bushy head of salt-and-pepper hair. It was said he'd taken Dante under his wing and taught him everything he knew.

The newly married couple and the wedding party and guests were gong to stay on board until the end of the cruise. Then they were to fly to Philadelphia for the more formal wedding.

Serena wondered with some amusement whether Ariana had followed through on her promise to wear her underpants inside out. Last evening Dante had had them all laughing when he recounted that particular piece of Italian folklore. Supposedly the bride needed to do this to keep *il malocchio,* the evil eye, away.

She must have chuckled out loud because Marc gently nudged her with his elbow. Serena became serious again. The minister had just asked if anyone objected to the marriage. After a moment of silence with no response, he and Captain Pappas jointly pronounced Dante and Ariana husband and wife.

Tears of joy streamed down Serena's cheeks. She wiped them away with the tissue Marc handed her. It had been a moving ceremony. The bride and groom had written their own vows and exchanged custom-made gold rings. They'd been through a tough time, but that had only made them closer. And it was evident that they were very much in love.

The wedding ceremony over, people began leaving the theater. Only a handful of passengers actually witnessing the wedding had been invited to the small reception. Serena, Pia and Marc were among them. Pia was being escorted by Andreas. Who knew how that relationship would end?

The guests followed a balloon lined path toward the Jasmine Spa. As they entered through a floral archway, Serena noted the outdoor Roman bath had been filled with white rose petals. More helium balloons floated from the columns. Staff members wandered around handing out little white boxes wrapped in tulle and guests were urged to open them.

"What's the significance of these favors?" Marc whispered, showing Serena the sugar-coated almonds that filled the interior of a miniature ship.

"I haven't a clue."

"Italians think almonds represent the bitter truth in life, and the sugar coating represents the hope for a happy future," another guest whispered.

"What a lovely tradition."

Serena swiped at her moist lids and swallowed the lump in her throat.

Marc gave her shoulders a squeeze. "I'm sure you must have some equally lovely Argentine traditions. You'll have to bring them out when we get married."

"Married?" She couldn't have heard him right. "Marc, are you proposing?"

He pulled out a folded piece of paper from his pocket. "I was saving this to read to you later." He cleared his throat. "'The Canadian Embassy is pleased to announce Mr. Marc LeClair has been re-instated in his Colombian post....'"

Serena threw her arms around him. "Marc, that's wonderful. You must be so excited."

"That's an understatement. How long will it take for you to plan a wedding?"

"Wedding? Marc, I live in Buenos Aires. My family's business is there."

"We'll work something out. And I can put in for a transfer down the road. If you'd like, I'll get down on my knees right now in front of everyone."

"Marc, shouldn't we talk about this some more? Long-distance relationships seldom work out."

"Just say yes. Say you'll love me forever. I'm crazy in love with you, and when two people love each other, anything is possible."

She took a deep breath. They'd make it work somehow.

"Yes, I want to marry you. Yes, I love you."

And she would prove it to him. Maybe they could commute, or even telecommute. Maybe her parents would consider opening a satellite office in Colombia. One way or another they would be together.

Champagne was now being poured and a delicious looking liqueur-soaked cake passed around. Forks were being clinked against glasses and shouts of "kiss, kiss, kiss," rang out. The bride and groom dutifully kissed, then kissed again.

"Single ladies, please form a circle," the assistant cruise director announced. "It's time for the bride to throw her bouquet."

Marc urged Serena to join the circle of hopefuls. The bride, spotting Serena, leapt from her seat and came bounding over. She folded the pendant into Serena's palm.

"Thank you so much for lending me the pendant. I hope you find a love of your own." She kissed Serena on both cheeks, continental style.

"I already have," Serena whispered back. "I already have."

Marc's hands cupped her shoulders.

"She's got me," he said. "And I don't plan on going anywhere."

The bride threw her bouquet in the direction of

her mother, who caught it. Elias Stamos kissed Sadie smack on the lips for all to see.

Tears of happiness misted Serena's eyes. When Selena died, she'd felt lost and incomplete. Marc had come along and somehow managed to fill that void. He loved her and had proved it by walking away from her in order to keep her safe.

Across the room, Pia gave her the thumbs-up sign.

Serena turned back to Marc, her heart in her eyes.

"This calls for a celebration. Shall we go to your stateroom?"

"I thought you would never ask." Marc kissed her soundly. "This is the best day of my life."

"Mine, too," Serena said, falling in step with him. "I can't wait to meet my new brother-in-law. I've always enjoyed being a twin."

"We'll have twins of our own," Marc answered, stopping to kiss her again.

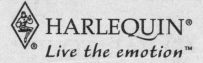

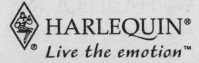

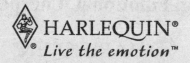

HARLEQUIN®
SuperRomance®

...there's more to the story!

Superromance.
A *big* satisfying read about unforgettable
characters. Each month we offer *six* very different
stories that range from family drama to adventure
and mystery, from highly emotional stories to
romantic comedies—and much more! Stories
about people you'll believe in and care about.
Stories too compelling to put down....

Our authors are among today's *best* romance
writers. You'll find familiar names and talented
newcomers. Many of them are award winners—
and you'll see why!

If you want the biggest and best
in romance fiction, you'll get it
from Superromance!

Exciting, Emotional, Unexpected...

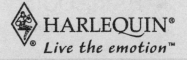

HARLEQUIN®
Live the emotion™

Silhouette®

Silhouette® SPECIAL EDITION™

Emotional, compelling stories that capture the intensity of living, loving and creating a family in today's world.

Silhouette® Desire

Modern, passionate reads that are powerful and provocative.

Silhouette® nocturne

Dramatic and sensual tales of paranormal romance.

Silhouette® Romantic SUSPENSE

Romances that are sparked by danger and fueled by passion.